Thumbprint Mysteries

THE HARD TIME CAFE

BY

STEPHEN F. WILCOX

D1407734

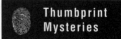

CB

CONTEMPORARY BOOKS

a division of NTC/CONTEMPORARY PUBLISHING GROUP
Lincolnwood, Illinois USA

Thumbprint
Mysteries

MORE THUMBPRINT MYSTERIES

by Stephen F. Wilcox:

Purgatory Prayers
The Hidden Men

This is a work of fiction. The characters, incidents, and dialogues are products of the author's imagination and are not to be construed as real. Any resemblance to actual events or persons, living or dead, is entirely coincidental.

Cover Design: Adam Niklewicz

ISBN: 0-8092-0602-1

Published by Contemporary Books,
a division of NTC/Contemporary Publishing Group, Inc.,
4255 West Touhy Avenue,
Lincolnwood (Chicago), Illinois 60646-1975 U.S.A.

890 QB 0 9 8 7 6 5 4 3 2 1

CHAPTER 1

A weak winter sun was setting along the city's western skyline. Two men stood in an alley off Carson Avenue, their faces hidden in the long shadows of Corpus Christi Catholic Church. One was tall and broad, dressed in a shabby tan raincoat. The other was smaller, slight, wearing dark clothing and a matching frown. In his hand was an envelope. He held it out, along with a warning.

"This had better be the end of it."

"Look at it this way." The tall man smiled. "It's just one more act of charity."

"Damn you to hell—" the other began, but the tall man cut him off.

"Now, now, such language. And from a priest yet."

* * *

1

It was past nine o'clock, and Mercy House was closed for the night. The managing staff was sitting around the dining room's big center table, nibbling leftover nachos and arguing.

"Shorter hours!" Billboard, who was the head chef, gave Father Joe a look. "With all due respect, Father, bullfeathers. If we shorten up the hours, we've got fewer jobs to fill. And if we've got fewer jobs, we can't bring in enough new cons to make a difference."

Sister Matthew nodded her head, her short hair moving in one piece like a brunette helmet. "He's right, Father. How can we possibly reduce our hours and still meet our goals?"

Father Joe Costello shrugged. "I know, I know. But we're facing a twenty percent cut in our budget. What else can we do?"

"Gotta be *somethin'* else," growled Reuben Macky, the restaurant's operations manager. "Maybe we could spice up the menu, add some Cajun or Thai dishes. We bring in more business, we make more money. Then we wouldn't need so much help from the Church and the charities."

"Ain't nothin' wrong with my menu, man," Billboard said in his country drawl. "What we need's a good gimmick. Somethin' to bring in the carriage trade, know what I mean? Valet parking maybe, so's they don't have to walk so far from the parking lot. This ain't exactly the best neighborhood."

"Right," Macky snorted. "We're gonna get the uptown crowd in here by havin' 'em turn their fancy cars over to ex-cons for safekeeping. Like they don't already think this joint's a front to rip them off somehow." He drew on his cigarette. "A liquor license is what we really need. Just for beer and wine would be good."

Sister Matty tut-tutted. *"That* definitely isn't our mission, encouraging drinking." She glanced at Father Joe but he was staring at the tabletop. "Besides," she went on, "we all know the state liquor authority would never give us a license."

"Well, hell—'scuse me, Matty—but we gotta come up with *something*."

Everyone agreed, and then everyone went silent, searching their thoughts for a good idea. The quiet in the dining hall was unnerving, as if Mercy House had already sunk under its debts and closed its doors. Father Joe seemed especially unhappy, but then he hadn't been his usual cheerful self all day.

Sister Matthew, watching him, was trying to think of something positive to say when one of the others slapped the tabletop.

"Theme the place." It was the new guy, Chester Tomzak. These were almost the first words Tomzak had said since beginning his parole three weeks before. That in itself was enough to grab everyone's attention. Tomzak had been the night manager of a tavern before he served four years at Arcadia for manslaughter.

"Theme?" Billboard said. "Like—how do you mean?"

Tomzak was bobbing his head, looking around the table. Then he uncoiled his wiry body from his chair and began to pace. "I mean come up with a theme, man. For the decor, the menu, the uniforms the waiters wear. Everything. Like they do at those chain restaurants. You got your Tex-Mex barbecue joints, your fake English pubs, your Aussie down-under steak houses. That's what we need. A theme!"

"Yeah," Macky smirked. "Like we'll call ourselves Thank God It's Paroleday."

"No, how 'bout somethin' French," Billboard jumped in, "like Le Pen."

He was grinning, as were the others. Except for Father Joe, who was only half listening. And Chester Tomzak, who was serious.

"Those names aren't bad," he told Macky and Billboard. "Only I was thinking we could call the place The Hard Time Cafe. Put bars over the windows, have private cells instead of booths. Maybe even have the waiters wear striped prison outfits, like Elvis in *Jailhouse Rock*. That could be our theme song."

Billboard snickered. "Yeah, and I suppose we serve up shit-on-a-shing . . . oh, uh, sorry, Matty. I meant to say creamed chipped beef on toast."

"You're forgiven, William," the sister said. Billboard's real name was William Lee Ralston. Everyone called him Billboard because of the prison tattoos that covered his arms and chest. Everyone except Sister Matty. "You're really serious, aren't you, Chester?"

"Yes, ma'am, I sure am." He sat down again. "Look, Macky is right. People with money in their pockets are afraid to come to Mercy House. Or they hear about a bunch of ex-cons running a restaurant, and they figure who needs it? I gave at the office, right? What I'm saying is they think of us as some halfway house. Make-work for parolees. Not as a place to come to eat and have a good time."

"You have a point, Chester. But to call the restaurant The Hard Time Cafe—isn't that demeaning to the men we're trying to help?"

"I'm one of those men and it doesn't bother me. How about you guys?"

The other two ex-cons looked at each other and shrugged.

"Don't bother me none."

"Losing this place, now *that* would be demeaning."

Tomzak turned back to Sister Matty. "It's called making chicken salad out of chicken—uh, feathers, ma'am. Everybody knows what this place is about. We can't hide it. So why not go with it?"

Once again Sister Matty looked at Father Joe, who was still staring down at the tabletop. She and the others joined him in a silence that went on for several seconds. A bare silver maple branch scratching at one of the high windows was the only sound. Outside, a chilly late February breeze blew along Carson Avenue.

Finally Reuben Macky broke the spell.

"I don't know about the rest of you," he said, a smile spreading across his deep brown face. "But I think I like it. The Hard Time Cafe."

"It does grow on you."

"How's this?" Billboard said. "We make the front of the menus look like an arrest warrant."

"Yeah, and we call the house dressing the 'big house' dressing. And you know the fancy places have that velvet rope across the entrance to the dining room? We could use handcuffs."

"Oh, here's a thought, gentlemen. We could decorate the walls with framed movie posters from famous prison films. Like *White Lightning, The Birdman of Alcatraz.*"

"*Escape from Alcatraz.* Everybody likes Clint Eastwood."

"*The Shawshank Redemption.*"

"Just a minute." Father Joe suddenly came back to the present. He stroked his short red beard. "Um, haven't we gotten a bit off the subject, people, gabbing away about movies? We're here to discuss our budget problems, after all."

They all stared at him, then began to laugh. A chuckle at first, then in uncontrolled laughter. Before things calmed down even Father Joe was chuckling, although he didn't know why.

"It's this idea Chester had, Father," said Sister Matthew. "To theme Mercy House around—oh, why don't you explain it, Chester."

"Well, sure. Okay." Tomzak stood up again and began to pace.

Father Joe was a hard sell at first. It took another twenty minutes of going over the same ground, but this time Tomzak had help. The others were firmly behind the idea now. Father Joe could see he was outvoted.

"Well, I still don't like it," he said at last. "But since this *is* a democracy—I guess Mercy House Restaurant is about to become The Hard Time Cafe."

*   *   *

The tall man sat on a stool near the front window at O'Mara's Tavern on Braun Street. From there he could see the side entrance to Corpus Christi Church, as well as the rectory.

He'd been drinking for hours, nursing Jim Beam while munching on bar snacks. The booze was taking hold. The cocky front he had put on for the priest was gone now. He felt fear tingling his nerve ends. He knew the game he was playing could put him right back in prison again.

"Nothing ventured, nothing gained," he mumbled into his glass.

Across the street a single light came on in a second-floor window of the rectory. A shape moved across the drawn shade like a spirit. The tall man shook off the image and took another swallow. It would be okay. A perfect setup. His old friend, the priest, wouldn't—couldn't—turn him in.

Not even when he went back for seconds.

CHAPTER 2

Sister Matthew couldn't believe her eyes. It was fifteen minutes before the grand opening, and already there was a line stretching for half a block down Carson Avenue.

A line!

She crossed herself and said a silent prayer. It had taken a month to change Mercy House into The Hard Time Cafe. A month of long hours and sometimes short tempers. Hours of painting and hammering, and meeting after meeting with the parish board or the city zoning people.

Now the converted storefront had been converted a second time, from a low-key Italian-style restaurant with checked tablecloths to a Hollywood ideal of a prison mess hall. The walls were painted gray, with just enough black accents to provide shadow lines. It proved too expensive to put real bars on the windows, so they'd

7

been painted on using black paint. Blues music poured from ceiling speakers. Framed posters from prison pictures formed a gallery along one wall.

The overall effect wasn't really like a prison, of course. It was more like a TV sitcom version of jail. But the suggestion was there and, besides, it was the parolees themselves who would be the real stars of the show.

The little nun took another glance through the front door's glass at the growing line.

"Dear Lord," she murmured, "let us be ready."

Reuben Macky rushed up to her with Billboard in his shadow. Like all the other employees, they were dressed in jeans and blue cotton workshirts with their names stenciled above the left breast pocket. The idea of wearing old-style striped prison uniforms had been voted down.

"We got a problem, Matty," Macky said. "No spoons."

"No spoons?"

"Not *no* spoons," Billboard corrected. "Just not enough. You know the new flatware we ordered? They sent about three times as many forks and knives as spoons."

"Yeah, and with that crowd out there . . ." Macky didn't bother to complete the thought.

In the years she'd worked with them, she had never known either of these big, tough ex-cons to worry about anything. Now they were fussing over spoons. She had to look up to make eye contact. "Calm down, gentlemen. We'll make do. If need be, we can break out the old flatware to get more spoons."

That seemed to satisfy them for the moment, and they headed back to the kitchen.

Sister Matty shook her head. It seemed that everyone from Father Joe on down was nursing a case of nerves these days. Everyone except Chester Tomzak, that is. She looked across the empty dining room to the salad bar. Tomzak was calmly sampling a piece of lettuce for freshness.

She had seen all kinds come through Mercy House. Most were young men when they went to prison. Boys, many of them, paying the price for a bad upbringing, making bad choices. Years behind bars had taken the shine off most of them. They hadn't matured, they had surrendered, Sister Matty thought.

But Chester Tomzak was different. The other men could see it, but they didn't know why. Sister Matty did. She had read Tomzak's file and had sat in on his parole hearing with Father Joe. So she knew about his middle-class upbringing. She knew about his college education and his stable work record and the family he once had. Most important, she knew about the single mistake in his life. The mistake that had sent him to prison and turned him into this quiet, private soul.

One more thing she knew: that some of the men resented Tomzak already. They mistook his pain for snobbery. If they only knew more, she thought . . .

But, no. It wasn't her place. The men's backgrounds were private, unless they chose to talk themselves. So far, Chester Tomzak had chosen not to. Sister Matty only hoped it wouldn't lead him to more problems.

*   *   *

The doors opened at 11:30 sharp for the lunch crowd. The rest of the day was a blur for the staff of The Hard Time Cafe. It was an odd mix, burly men in prison clothes working their way through groups of business people in pinstripes and the tweed crowd from the university. Trays held high and loaded with orders of big house salads and yardbird stew, soup du jail and prime(rib) offender sandwiches.

The first small lull in the action came around two o'clock. Tomzak decided to grab five minutes for a cup of coffee. He went out the delivery door at the back of the cramped kitchen, steaming mug in hand. It was then that he saw Father Joe coming up the alley.

Some fifty feet farther on, moving off in the other direction, was another man. Tall, broad in the shoulders, a tan raincoat flapping behind him; these were the things Tomzak would remember later.

"Hello, Chet," the priest said as he came nearer. "Grabbing a moment's peace?"

"Yeah, exactly." He sipped his coffee. "It looks like we're a hit."

"Well, let's hope. Not that we can base much on the first day. I mean, the novelty factor and all that."

"Shows uptown people are willing to come down here, though. I see a lot of yuppies in there. Like you say, we'll need to keep them coming . . ." He paused. The priest seemed to be looking through him, not hearing. "Are you okay, Father?"

"What?" He blinked at Tomzak as he absently stroked his beard. "Forgive me, Chet. A thousand things on my mind, I'm afraid."

"It looks like you could use a few minutes of R and R yourself. Let me buy you a cup?"

"Best offer I've had today," Father Costello said, and they returned to the heat and hurry of the kitchen.

*   *   *

By a quarter to nine that evening, the dining room was nearly empty. A few customers lingered over coffees and dessert. The staff was busy clearing tables, setting up for the next day. From the ceiling speakers came the Bobby Fuller Four singing "I Fought the Law and the Law Won."

"Man," said Billboard, flopping into a chair at a corner table. "Wring me out and hang me up to dry! I'm flat wore out."

"I hate to admit it," Reuben Macky said, "but you didn't do half bad for a redneck peckerwood. Burnt hell outa that one order of eggplant parmesan, but other than that—"

"That's 'cause I mistook that eggplant for your shiny purple head, you son of a—"

"Boys." It was all Sister Matty needed to say. She'd gotten used to their banter over the years, just as they had gotten used to having her play referee. "William, your food was excellent. You and your crew should be proud."

"Thank you, ma'am."

"And Reuben, it was like watching a ballet, how you and Chester kept everything flowing smoothly. I don't think anyone had to wait more than fifteen minutes for a table. And the waiters got the orders served in good time." She laughed. "Even with the customers talking their ears off."

"Ain't it the truth," Macky nodded. "I had to wait a couple of tables myself to fill in when Ernie and Donzell took breaks. Somebody asked if we're real ex-cons, like this is some kind of put-on."

Billboard snickered. "Anybody ask you what you were in for?"

"Only about six times," Macky said. "I told this one hotshot I killed a guy for invading my privacy."

"Reuben! You didn't!"

"Hey, Sister, these folks want a taste of life inside? Fine. First thing you learn is you don't get in a man's face unless you're ready for him to come back on you. My time is my time. I don't need someone in a suit trying to get off on me to impress the ladies." In a flash, his mood went from boil to simmer. "I mean, I got the feeling some of these fine citizens think we're talking robots or something, like at Disneyland."

Billboard barked out a laugh. "Yeah, or like that clown you holler your order into at Jack in the Box."

"It doesn't hurt to set 'em straight every so often."

"Yes, but we don't want to scare the public away—"

"Aw, it wasn't a big deal, Sister. The rest of the guy's table knew I was jerking his chain. The little secretaries got a giggle out of it, anyway."

Sister Matthew let the matter drop. If she had learned anything over the years, it's that you don't push, not on the small stuff. The parolees had a sense of themselves that only another ex-con could fully understand. Just like men who have been in combat, she thought. Or, for that matter, policemen. People who have seen the underside of life from close up and lived to tell about it.

That was another reason some of the men resented Chester Tomzak. By not joining in the kidding and the tall tales the others told about their prison experiences, he was shutting them out. As if saying thanks for the invitation, but I'm not interested in belonging to your club.

Or perhaps Sister Matty was exaggerating the problem. She wouldn't put it past herself. She remembered one of her favorite Bible verses, Luke 15, the parable of the lost sheep. She was too much a mother to her flock, perhaps. But if it was good enough for Jesus, well . . .

She looked around the nearly deserted dining room. "Has anyone seen Chester, by the way?"

"He was inventorying the stock in the storeroom last I saw him. Trying to make the rest of us look bad."

"Hah," Billboard snorted. "That wouldn't surprise me none."

*   *   *

Indeed, Chester Tomzak had just left the storeroom, clipboard in hand. He was making a note to order more napkins. For the second time that day he saw Father Joe out in the alley.

Curious.

He watched for a moment through the window in the kitchen's back door. Father Joe was walking away from the restaurant down the shadowy alley. Carrying something in his left hand? Hard to tell at that distance what it was, but something.

He couldn't say what made him follow the priest. It was dark out in the alley and Father Costello, for all his years of working with hardened men, was still innocent. Call it a feeling, or a hunch. Whatever it was, it was enough for Tomzak to put aside his clipboard and hurry out the kitchen's back door.

CHAPTER 3

Father Joe Costello tried to do the math in his head as he walked. Let's see, a dozen parolees working at Mercy House. No, it's The Hard Time Cafe. Must remember the new name, now that it seems to be a hit.

Anyway, that's a dozen men. Plus four more parolees working for The Loaves & Fishes, the church's soup kitchen and free food pantry. Then there was the salary for Mrs. Hargaty, who managed The Loaves & Fishes as well as Peter's Closet, the secondhand clothing store. Last but hardly least was the Corpus Christi Friends Day Care. It was a co-operative, staffed by parent volunteers. But Ms. Palumbo, the teacher, was a certified professional and had to be paid as such.

That was about it. Eighteen people on the payroll. All the rest were volunteers. Parishioners with time to give and generous hearts. Of course, there were himself and Sister Matthew. And Father Sierra, the assistant pastor,

14

and old Mrs. Clooney, the rectory's housekeeper. But they were all paid from the church's approved budget. The others' pay—the eighteen—had to come out of the earnings from the restaurant and the clothing store, as well as the grant from the diocese.

The grant, Father Joe reminded himself, that had grown smaller in the last two years.

His heavy sigh echoed from the alley walls. There was so much *need* out there, and so little they could do. Eighteen men placed through the prison outreach program. Thirty-five kids in the day care program—all the state would allow without another certified teacher on staff. A hundred free meals a day provided by the soup kitchen. A few dozen families clothed and fed each month.

Drops in the bucket.

Which made his betrayal weigh that much heavier on his mind.

The zipper pouch with the money inside slapped against his trouser leg. The money the men had earned with their sweat, money needed to continue the parolee program and all the other good works at Corpus Christi. And yet, here he was, about to steal from his own flock. Again.

No! There had to be some other way.

He stopped and looked around, searching for an answer in the brick walls of the alley. It was a shortcut over to the rectory. Like Carson Avenue itself, the alley took a sharp bend about a block down, then straightened.

Beyond the bend. That was where they'd agreed to meet.

Father Joe slapped the money pouch against his leg and sighed again. *Lord, give me courage for what I must do.*

*   *   *

Tomzak didn't like night in the city. Too many bad memories. Too many bad old habits whispering to him from the shadows. It was fear, yes, but not the usual city fears. It was himself he feared. His old self. The one who had let booze and selfishness ruin the life he'd once taken for granted.

City life, night life. They had once been his world, but that world had come tumbling down on him. He wouldn't go back to it. Couldn't—

But he knew that was a lie. He *could* fall back into old habits, all too easily. Even knowing how much it had cost him the first time.

Thoughts of Emmy flashed across his brain. And Susan. A photo, the pair of them digging dirt in the backyard garden on Briar Lane. Mother and daughter. Family. The image was like a knife thrust at his heart. He blocked it by remembering what had brought him to the alley.

Concentrate on the priest. Father Joe. What was up with him, anyway? It was the parolees who were supposed to be moody, not the program director. And yet, here was Father Joe, the day of their grand re-opening, pacing behind the scenes.

Well, maybe he'd ask him what the deal was, if he ever caught up to him.

*   *   *

The tall man in the shabby raincoat rocked from one foot to the other. The cold and damp of the alley seemed to soak through the soles of his shoes. Spring nights were like that up here, he reminded himself. The sun goes down and takes with it every blessed ray of warmth.

Lucky he brought along a space heater.

He chuckled soundlessly as he drew the bottle from the coat's deep pocket. Many times he'd been able to fit half of everything he owned in these pockets. But those hard times just might be over. If . . .

He took a swallow of the Jim Beam. And another. Feeling better already. Now, what was he thinking? Oh, yeah. The priest. If the priest didn't give him any trouble.

"Goddamn priests anyway," he muttered. "Pushin' me around my whole life, seems like. Hell with all goddamn priests." And he took another swig.

A shudder ran through his wide shoulders. He leaned back against the brick wall. Farther along the wall, a floodlight shined down. He was barely within its glow.

Like the planet Neptune, a cold and distant world. The thought just popped into his head. A leftover, he supposed, from that good Jesuit education he'd almost received long ago. The solar system, your catechism, geometry; all drilled into you with the business end of a wooden ruler.

Just as the image formed in his head, a man dressed in jeans and a clerical collar rounded the corner. Father Joe Costello. Walking fast, head down, man on a mission. Swinging that money pouch, oh, yeah.

"My personal savior," the tall man growled. Costello had just better not give him any more shit. No more words.

Because he was not in a goddamn listening mood.

*   *   *

First were the angry noises. Tomzak could hear them coming from beyond the alley's bend. A kind of roar, a yell, a garbled curse, and another yell. By then he was around the corner in time to see the last blow fall.

"Hey! What the hell—?"

Again, first impressions: Tall man, tan raincoat, arm swinging an arc. A huddled figure on the ground. Father Joe! Then a shout—Tomzak himself, he realized—a curse, a shriek of shattering glass. Then the tall man running away, out of the light and into the darkness.

All of this happening in an eye-blink. And then Tomzak was at Father Joe's side, kneeling next to him. Not even feeling the broken glass cut into his knee or the smell of Jim Beam as it soaked into his jeans. The kindly priest was crumpled like a used newspaper. His legs were curled up and a stream of blood ran down the side of his face, turning his short red beard to copper. His eyes rolled beneath their nearly closed lids.

"Father Joe! Father, can you hear me?"

Tomzak was on both knees now. So much damn blood. He used the sleeve of his shirt to dab some of it away from Father Joe's left eye, but it did no good. It kept pouring down from his scalp, as if his head had been cracked wide open.

Oh, dear Jesus!

In the first moment of panic, he was lost. He had no idea what to do. Then, with a few deep breaths, some control began to return. He needed help. An ambulance. He started to rise.

The money pouch.

It was the first he'd noticed it. Father Joe had it cradled in his arms like an infant.

Tomzak looked up, glanced all around. What to do? Take another breath.

All right, Chet. You can't help Father Joe on your knees. Secure the money, run for help. Do it!

He leaned across the priest to grab the pouch. That's when he felt the broken glass of the whiskey bottle dig into his knee. He grunted in pain and let go of the pouch. He couldn't break Father Joe's grip, even with him unconscious. He got up, stood spread-legged over the fallen man for leverage, and leaned over. He pulled at the pouch, pulled again—and it came free.

"Hey! What the—? You son of a bitch!"

He heard feet pounding up the alley and began to turn. Halfway around, a blow struck his shoulder, sending him head over heels. He ended up in a heap at the base of the alley wall.

"I oughta kill you, you bastard!"

Tomzak blinked to clear the cobwebs and the night from his eyes. Billboard was standing over him, looking like he could stomp him into the paving stones. Others were rapidly coming up behind him; Macky, a couple of the waiters, some of the kitchen crew.

"Aw, Christ. Ernie, run back and call 911. Move your lazy ass!" Macky, taking charge. "Billboard, back off, man."

"Back off, shit. You see what he done—?"

"No, I didn't see what went down here and neither did you, so back off! This ain't the yard at Arcadia, man. Let the cops sort this thing out."

"Yeah. Right." Billboard began to turn, then swiftly came back around, sending a foot into Tomzak's side. While Tomzak rolled away, retching, Macky and one of the others got armlocks on the wiry ex-biker.

"Aw right already." Billboard stopped struggling. "I'm cool."

Macky got in his face. "Any more stomping gets done around here, hillbilly, you gonna be the stompee, you got that? You think this is what Father Joe wants, us poundin' the piss outa each other in some alley?"

"You made your point, superfly, okay?"

Macky felt Billboard's shoulders relax and he let him go.

"What about him?" Billboard said, jerking his head at Tomzak.

Macky walked over to where Tomzak lay holding his ribs. He bent over him and, ignoring Tomzak's outstretched hand, he took the money pouch.

"I know how this looks, Macky," Tomzak said, slowly getting to his feet, "but it wasn't me."

"Save it for the cops. Right now I got bigger things on my mind."

They joined the others gathered around the injured priest. One of the waiters, Donzell Jepson, had stripped off his T-shirt and was using it to mop away some of the blood.

"Careful, man. Don't put no pressure on that head wound. Could be he's got a skull fracture."

"Where the hell's that ambulance?"

"Ernie went to call 'em."

"So where the hell's Ernie? Jesus, he looks like he's dying here."

"He's breathing okay. That's something, anyway."

Just then Ernie rounded the corner with Sister Matty coming up behind him as fast as her short legs would take her. She was carrying an olive green army blanket and the first aid kit from the kitchen. One look, however, and she knew Father Joe couldn't be helped with Band-Aids and iodine.

She carefully spread the blanket over him and got down beside him. "All right, don't move him. All we can do is keep him warm. The paramedics will be here any moment."

She looked up. Her eyes swept the faces of the men circled around her, noting their concern, their fears. When she came to Chet Tomzak, she paused. He felt her gaze reach deep down inside him.

He shook his head. "I swear to God it wasn't me, Sister. There was another man, a tall man . . ."

But he stopped in mid-sentence. Sister Matty's head had gone back down to Father Joe, her hands pressed together, her lips moving in quiet prayer. Soon the others joined in, each man mumbling his own words, a babble of hope.

Tomzak pinched his eyes shut and joined in, just as the whine of distant sirens pierced the night air.

CHAPTER 4

"I'm telling you, it comes down to the 'R' word."

"The R word?" Sergeant Greene nodded. "Oh, you mean 'ridiculous'?"

"Ha, ha, ha." Sergeant Hafner laughed but he was not amused.

"Okay. I believe 'recidivism' is what you're going for."

"Right. Recid—recid—" Hafner gripped the steering wheel as if to strangle it. "Oh, however the hell you say it. 'Repeat offenders' is what it means. Repeaters are the heart of the crime problem in this city and this state and this country. And that's why I don't think much of prison outreach programs."

Greene glanced over at his partner from the passenger's seat of their vanilla Ford. "You simply don't believe in rehabilitation, then."

"For buildings, yes; for perps, no. For cons I believe in a couple other R words: revenge and restitution." He smiled, pleased with himself.

"Lock 'em up and throw away the key, huh?"

"If you can't execute 'em, yeah."

"So you're gonna give a life stretch to a car thief?"

"Course not. Don't be dense."

"Check kiter? Burglar? College kid caught with a lit doobie at a rock concert?"

"No, no, no. C'mon, Kel, you know what I mean. Hardcore guys. Capital offenders. Career criminals. There's no changing those scumbags. Keep 'em off the streets and crime drops sixty, seventy percent. You've seen the numbers."

"Oh, ho!" Now it was Greene's turn to laugh. "The numbers? I thought you're the guy who always says statistics lie."

"Well, there are statistics and statistics," Hafner said. "As everybody knows."

"Yeah, right, Harold."

They settled into an easy silence. The pair had been partners for seven years. They were like an old married couple who had grown comfortable with their differences. The least of their differences was race.

Harold Hafner, older by a decade, was a basic shoe-leather cop who had come up through the ranks. He was a throwback in every way, from his love of Frank Sinatra records to his methods as a police detective. He believed if you pounded on enough doors—and enough suspects—you could close almost any case.

Kelvin Greene, on the other hand, was a college man with a degree in sociology. He was big on motive and on developing profiles of suspects in major cases. It drove his partner up the wall, of course, but that's half the reason he did it.

Hafner turned the unmarked Ford off East Main and onto Carson Avenue. "Tell you what. You wanna bet me ten bucks that whatever went down over at Corpus Christi *wasn't* the work of one of Costello's cons?"

"Betting is against the law, as you well know," Greene said.

"Hah!"

"Besides," Greene added, "just because I'm open-minded doesn't mean I'm stupid."

They sped past the church and continued for another block. At Tyson Place, Hafner took a quick left and followed the narrow street to the end. Running off in either direction was the alley. Up to the right, near where the alley doglegged, was a green and white ambulance.

"Better leave the car here," Greene suggested. "Give the EMTs room to pull out."

His partner grunted agreement and switched off the car.

A small crowd had formed a half circle around the paramedics. *Jesus,* Hafner thought, looking around at the faces, *it looks like the wanted posters on a post office wall around here.* "Let's back it up, give the man some air." He tilted his head as he looked down at the man on the gurney. "Hey, it's Father Costello."

"Of course it is, officer. You didn't know that?"

Hafner looked at the little brown-haired woman who had abruptly appeared at his side and returned her frown. "We got a report of an assault involving Corpus Christi personnel, that's all. And it's *Sergeant*. Detective Sergeant Hafner." When the little woman nodded, he added, "And you are?"

"Sister Matthew. I'm assistant director of the prison outreach program at the church."

"Mmm. Nice to meet you, Sister." He tried not to stare at her jeans and baggy wool ski sweater. Even though he wasn't Catholic himself, Hafner preferred the old days when nuns wore habits, like Sally Field in that old TV show. At least you knew who you were talking to back then.

"So what happened here? Anybody see what went down?"

"Well, sergeant, we've just been discussing that—"

"Oh, you've been discussing that, have you? Getting your stories straight?"

"No, simply trying to make sense out of this tragedy." She turned to watch the EMTs carefully load the gurney into the ambulance. Father Joe was lying on his back, his head held steady with a vice-like device, a bandage taped loosely against his skull. His eyes were closed, his face gray and still.

"Making sense out of it is our job, Sister," Hafner said. While he had been talking with the munchkin nun, his partner had been questioning the others. Now Greene approached him, leading by the elbow an average-looking white guy with wispy blonde hair and sad eyes. Following along was another white guy, this one lanky, with receding hair and enough tattoos to get a job in a carnival sideshow.

Greene stopped the blonde man in front of Hafner and flipped open his notepad. "This is Chester Tomzak, one of the parolees. Says he saw the whole thing."

"Saw it!" Billboard stuck out his large goateed jaw. "You bet he saw it. He *done* it."

"That's a lie! I was trying to help—"

"Okay, girls, one at a time." Hafner aimed a stiff finger at Billboard's often-broken nose. "You. Don't I know you from some place?"

"William Lee Ralston. They call me Billboard. You, uh, busted me about fourteen years back."

"Yeah. Biker, right? Used to run with the Warlords?"

"That was a long time ago."

"Assault, right? And possession with intent?"

"Simple possession," Billboard said defensively. "And the assault got pleaded down to D&D. I ended up doin' half a buck at County is all." Half a buck was six months.

"That time," Hafner pressed. "But you must've gone upstate for a while after that. You've ended up with Father Costello's operation."

Billboard put on a weak smile. "DA wasn't too eager to talk the second time around."

"I'll get back to you. Stay put." Hafner switched his attention to Tomzak. Guy didn't look like he'd say boo on Halloween, but Hafner knew looks meant nothing. "What's his story?" he asked his partner.

Greene flipped back the pages of his notepad and read the key points aloud. "Chester Tomzak, business manager for the restaurant. Claimed to have seen a tall, broad-shouldered man in a tan raincoat assault the priest with a whiskey bottle. Chased the guy off, then tried to give assistance to the priest." He jerked a thumb at Billboard. "That's where things stood when this guy and some of the others came running."

While Greene was reading, Hafner kept his gaze on Tomzak's face. "This tall guy you claim you saw. You recognize him?"

"I didn't really *see* him. His face, I mean. It was more like a quick impression."

"So you couldn't ID him, say in a lineup?"

"Maybe. I doubt it." Tomzak's natural frown deepened. "I saw him before, though." He explained about seeing the man and Father Joe out in the alley earlier that day.

Greene said, "You think they were together out there for some reason?"

"It looked that way. I mean, they were both out there at the same time."

"Yeah," Greene said, "but it could be Father Costello was coming back from the rectory and this tall guy in the raincoat was just taking a shortcut someplace. Two ships passing in the night, so to speak. What made you think there was a connection?"

"I didn't think there was a connection at the time. I didn't think anything. Until I saw the same guy whacking Father Joe with that bottle."

Greene agreed with a quick nod of the head.

"So ask him why I found him standing over Joe, grabbin' the money from the restaurant," Billboard blurted.

"I was going to take it with me for safekeeping while I called an ambulance."

"You say."

Sister Matthew had been seeing the ambulance off. Now she edged her way back into the circle of men. "There *was* another man, like the one Chester saw. I noticed him too."

Greene turned to her. "This was out here in the alley, ma'am?"

"No, it was earlier. Sometime during the lunch hour rush. Let me think." Her hand went to her short brown hair, the fingers running through it like the teeth on a comb. "Yes. He was standing with a crowd of people at the front of the restaurant. A tall man, around forty to fifty, I'd say. Big through the shoulders. And wearing a raincoat."

"So he was with a group of customers waiting for a table, Sister?"

"Well, no. I think he was by himself, standing *near* some people who were waiting for a table. But I had the impression he was by himself."

"What made you notice this guy at all?" Hafner wanted to know. "I mean, if it was so busy in there, why'd this guy stand out?"

"Well, at first—" She hesitated, and Hafner was sure he detected a mild blush. "I suppose I noticed him because he looked a bit out of place. More like he should've been working at The Hard Time Cafe rather than coming in as a customer."

"You're saying this guy looked like rough trade, Sister? An ex-con?"

Now the blush came in full bloom. Hafner saw her sneak a glance at Tomzak and the others before answering. "I know I shouldn't judge a book by its cover, but—well, he just had a certain look about him. A wariness, you might say."

"Uh huh." Hafner made a note on his notepad. "Maybe eating in a place run by thieves and murderers is enough to make anybody a little cautious, you think?"

The others didn't rise to the bait, but Sister Matty did.

"That's uncalled for, sergeant." She gave him a glare, a look she hadn't used since giving up teaching social studies to Catholic school girls a decade earlier. Hafner looked down at her blankly.

"At any rate," she continued, "the man didn't stay to eat. That's the other reason I remembered him. I noticed he seemed to be staring across the room at something.

Or someone. I followed his gaze and realized he was watching Father Joe, who was helping bus tables. But when I looked back at this man, he was gone."

"Okay." Greene was nodding his head. "Let's see if we can separate the facts from the feelings here, Sister. You saw a man in the restaurant today who generally fits the description of the man Tomzak claims attacked Father Costello."

"Yes, and I'd say he more than generally matches Chester's description—"

"But what you *can't* say for sure is whether the man was alone or with others. You can't say whether he was really watching Father Costello for some reason."

"He was. He was staring across the room at him."

"Or staring at someone at the table the good father was bussing. Or maybe simply daydreaming, staring off into space while waiting for a table. Which was so slow in coming, he decided to go down the block to McDonald's instead. Isn't that just as likely, ma'am?"

Sister Matty sighed as she looked up into the dark face and calm brown eyes of Sergeant Greene. "I think you've made up your mind already not to believe what Chester told you, that's what I think." She switched to Hafner. "The both of you."

"Uh huh." Hafner tucked away his notepad. "Well, what I think is we'll take all three of you folks down to Metro. See if we can sort this thing out one way or another."

"I'll be along as soon as I can," Sister Matty said. "But right now I'm going to the hospital with Father Joe." Neither sergeant argued with her.

*   *   *

Metropolitan Police Headquarters shared space with the county jail and the Hall of Justice on the west side of

Riverton's downtown district. The huge building was a Cold War relic. It was built in the late 1950s out of foot-thick concrete. Below two floors of underground garages was a Civil Defense shelter big enough to protect fifteen hundred people from The Big One, the atomic bomb. In theory, anyway.

Sergeant Harold Hafner had always wondered which would be worse, dying from a nuclear attack or surviving down there in that dripping concrete coffin.

"Okey-dokey." He re-entered Interview Room 3 carrying a thin file folder and took a seat at the old scarred table. "Let's see what we've got on Mr. Chester W. Tomzak, shall we?"

Tomzak was seated across from Hafner, his elbows on the table, his hands clasping and unclasping in front of him. Greene, who had stayed with Tomzak while his partner searched out the man's sheet, remained standing.

"He ask for a lawyer yet?" Hafner asked, not taking his eyes off Tomzak.

"Nope," Greene said.

"Why should I need a lawyer? Are you charging me with something?"

"No. All we're doing is talking. For now, anyway."

"I've cooperated fully." Tomzak's hand went toward his left breast pocket; a reflex, reaching for the cigarettes he'd given up years before. "I told you what I saw."

"That's right, and we appreciate it. But what we're gonna do right now is we're gonna take a look at other possibilities." Hafner opened the file folder and, laying his palms flat on the table, looked down at the single yellow sheet it contained. "Hmm. Uh huh. Well, well."

He motioned to Greene, who came up behind him and read over his shoulder, making his own series of grunts. It was a routine they had performed scores of times.

"So, Chet—I can call you Chet, right? It says here you did four years at Calderwood for vehicular homicide. Four years, for a first-time offense? Jesus! Who'd you have for a lawyer, Jerry Lewis? My mother could've pleaded you out for eighteen months and an alcohol rehab program."

"I did the crime, I did the time. That's all."

"Wow. Hey, Kel, fire up the theme from *Baretta*, why don'tcha? I think we got ourselves a hero here."

Greene pulled out a chair, put one foot up on the seat, then leaned on his elbow. "You copped a guilty plea, Chet? Went down for the whole count, huh?"

"Yes."

"That's guilt, all right," Hafner said. "Punish me, your honor, for I have sinned."

Greene said, "Says on your sheet you were responsible for two deaths. You were legally drunk. Way over, in fact, with a blood-alcohol count off the charts. You wanna give us the particulars, man?"

"There's not much to tell."

It was Tomzak's first and only lie. There was plenty to tell.

CHAPTER
5

It was a cold, snowy night almost five years ago. Tomzak was the manager of Wooly Bully's, an upscale tavern tucked in at street level in the Midtowner Hotel. It was located only six blocks from where he now sat staring at a couple of Metro detectives.

Back then, home was a Cape Cod-style house in Haddenfield, a quiet suburb south of the city. Home was his wife, Susan, and their six-year-old daughter, Emmy, and a golden retriever named Rex.

He was not the best of husbands, but he was far from the worst. His job was the main problem between him and Susan. He worked a lot of nights, often very late nights. He missed school events, parent-teacher meetings. It was the cause of most of their arguments, and the arguments had gotten worse.

First, he and Susan were barely speaking to one another outside of polite talk in front of Emmy. Then they weren't even sleeping together. He came home one morning at two A.M. and went to the guest bedroom, not wanting to wake up Susan. But she had taken it as rejection of her, and he'd been sleeping in that guest bed ever since.

That was the excuse he gave himself to stay at the bar too long that night and drink far too much. To feel sorry for himself. To forget about his wife and his child and what he owed them.

To not turn away when the redhead at the end of the bar asked him to join her.

He probably poured his heart out to the redhead, the usual cheater's excuse: my wife doesn't understand. It could've been a motto hung up over the tavern's mahogany bar, he'd heard it so many times from others. He imagined he'd used the same line himself that night, only he couldn't remember. He and the woman were both so drunk that the evening was reduced to a series of snapshots. Laughing together at the bar. Ushering her out the front door with a grand bow. Dropping his keys in the slush when he fumbled to unlock his car. Her lipstick smearing across his lips and cheek as they groped each other in the front seat.

The rest was a haze, until a few terrifying moments out on the Eastside Expressway brought everything into sharp focus.

The woman, laughing with him, pouring cognac from a flask down his throat while he drove as if in a dream.

The bleating of angry horns all around them.

Pairs of headlights, high beams flashing like accusing eyes, hurtling past.

That last set of lights coming head-on, stunning him.

And in that final quarter-second before impact,

realizing he was going the wrong way on a three-lane highway, through the slanting snow, in the dead of night.

The driver's airbag saved him. He remembered it punching him in the face and chest and being thankful for its protection. Then he took in the horror around him and wished with all his heart there had been no airbag. Wished he'd died right then and there and gotten it over with.

There was no airbag on the passenger's side. The redhead lay half out the front of the car, her face having shattered the windshield. She was still alive, moaning, and she would live. For better or worse, she would live.

The couple in the other car would not. The husband was already dead by the time Tomzak managed to stagger to the side of their crumpled Toyota. His wife—her name was Cathy, Tomzak later learned—lived long enough to scream out her pain and her loss. To lift her disbelieving eyes from the bloody remains of her husband. To see Tomzak's slack, drunken face staring down at her through the car's cracked windshield.

It was a look she would take to her grave, and that Tomzak would take to his as well.

Now he stared across the table at the two detectives and said evenly, "I got drunk one night and ran into another car on the expressway. The man and woman in the other car were killed, and the woman riding with me was badly injured. That's it."

"It eats at you, doesn't it?" Hafner said.

"What do you think?"

"Yeah, I can see. Regret, guilt, sorrow, it's all etched into your face." He leaned across the table, his voice barely above a whisper. "And maybe anger, too, huh, Chester? Like, why'd it have to happen to me? One misstep. One really bad night on the town and it cost you, what? Your freedom, your good name, your job. Your family too, I'll bet."

Tomzak's eyes flickered angrily, then shifted away.

"You were married, right, Chester? Had kids? What was it, one or two? But you screw up one night and that's that. The wife divorces you, takes the kids with her. Nobody to visit you for four long years in the can. She's probably remarried by now, your kids calling some other guy Daddy. She remarried now, Chester?"

Tomzak pounded his fist on the table. "Yes! Yes, she's remarried! All of it, okay?" He felt a dull throbbing in his bones, as if he'd been beaten from head to toe. "For God's sake, why are you doing this to me?"

"We're just trying to get at the truth here, Chester."

"I've told you the truth!"

"Maybe you have, Chet." Like a well-rehearsed dance, Greene sat down and Hafner stood and moved away from the table. Time for the good cop to work. "You've got your version of events, sure. But we're paid to look at all the possibilities. You understand that, don't you?"

"I guess. But my . . . background doesn't have anything to do with it."

"Well," Greene dipped his head to the side, "let's think about that for a minute. We've got your buddy Billboard over in I-Room 1 giving a statement. All about how he and some of the others were in the kitchen there at The Hard Time Cafe, wondering where you and the good father had gone to. So Billboard decides to go out looking, see if you'd headed over to the church for some reason. Then he's coming up the alley, and he hears some shouting. When he clears the corner, there you are, taking that money pouch away from Father Joe—"

"I've explained that."

"Yeah, I know. The tall man. And I tend to believe you on that. But there is this other possibility we have to check out."

Tomzak waited as long as he could, trying to hold Greene's brown-eyed stare before giving in. "Which is?"

That was Hafner's cue. He charged back to the table like a rodeo bull. "Which is you got a big chip on your shoulder, Chester. The world screwed you, taking away that nice suburban life of yours for one lousy mistake. *God* screwed you. He plunked you down in the middle of a no-win situation and then sat back to watch you squirm. Took away every blessed thing you ever had and put your ass in a jail cell for four years.

"But you know the cruelest part of the joke God played on you, Chester? After putting you into that situation in the first place? And then making you pay for your guilt for four years, giving up your family, your career? You know what He did then?"

Greene picked it up. "He paroled you to a bunch of true believers. 'God is good. Merciful Jesus. By our faith we shall know ye.' Landed you flat in the middle of a bunch of bleeding-heart priests and nuns. Now that's what I call irony, Chet."

"Didn't you want to ask them every day?" Hafner said. "I mean, I would. Like, 'Hey, Father Joe, if God has a plan, if He sees all, if it's all His will, why's He picking on me?' That's what I'd wanna know."

Greene chuckled. "I'll bet he'd say something like, 'Oh, but it's not up to us mortals to question God's reasoning.' Is that how Father Joe tried to explain it, Chet—?"

Tomzak was shaking his head. "You guys are nuts."

"Because I can't imagine you wanna hear that from anybody, am I right?" asked Greene.

"Sure, you're right, Kel," Hafner came back. "Who the hell are these holy rollers, anyway, to fill a man's head with such crap. A man like Chester here, who *knows* there's no such thing as a merciful God, not for him anyway."

"Let me guess how it was, Chet." Greene's voice was silk now, soothing. "It's been a long hard day, the new restaurant theme was a success. But you're dog tired, man. And maybe you need a little nip too, huh? Got a pint of Jim Beam stashed in your jacket. So out you go, into the alley for some peace and quiet. Only along comes the priest, Father Joe."

"No—"

"He spots that bottle and he starts raggin' on you. How you need to be strong, take it one day at a time. How God will help—"

"No! It didn't happen that way," Tomzak protested.

"And maybe you just snapped, right then and there. No more of this God stuff, this God who'd abandoned you. You didn't even think about it, you just swung that bottle at the priest, and you swung it again."

"How many ways can I say it?" Tomzak asked. "No!"

"Aw, c'mon, Tomzak." Hafner jumped in. "Your biker buddy says you got a chip on your shoulder a mile wide. Think you're better than everybody down there. You're just waiting for a chance to blow off the program. Then along comes Father Costello, giving you a hard time about the booze, pissing you off. And dangling that money pouch, too. I mean, he was asking for it. Here was your big chance to get out—"

"Look, ask Father Joe. He'll tell you it wasn't me."

"We told you, Chet, Father Joe is still out. He's in a coma. For all we know he might never come out of it."

"In which case, Chester, you're looking at a murder rap."

"That's it." Tomzak half rose, then sat back down. "I want a lawyer. No more talk."

"Yeah, I can understand why you'd want a lawyer, Chester. Caught red-handed, smelling of whiskey, the priest with his head bashed in, and you holding the money."

"Give me a breath test! A blood test, a lie detector, any goddamn test you want! I didn't do anything wrong! Can you understand that? I didn't do anything!"

Chet Tomzak buried his face in his hands and cried softly. Silently, Greene and Hafner slipped out of I-Room 3. From the observation room next door, through the one-way mirror, they watched as Tomzak slowly pulled himself together. The clock on the wall behind them said it was twenty-nine minutes to eleven.

"So what d'you think?" Hafner said.

"I think we stepped on him pretty good and he didn't squeak." Greene ran a hand across his tired face and yawned. "I'd like him better for it if his sheet wasn't only a quarter page long. There's nothing there, except that one conviction."

"Yeah, maybe. But I still say this deal ties in with one of Costello's cons. And Tomzak's the one who got caught holding the bag. Literally."

"Could be it went down like he said it did. When the priest comes around—if he comes around—he could clear Tomzak."

"Anything's possible, I suppose." Hafner glanced at the wall clock. "The question for right now is, do we get him a lawyer or cut him loose? And don't say cut him loose, because I don't want to do that. This guy's got every reason in the world to run on us."

"I don't know. He's been pretty cooperative so far."

"Sure, but don't forget the guy's got another fifteen

months of parole. He knows if he stops acting like he's cooperating, we could violate him to his parole officer."

"Well, maybe. Anyway, we haven't got enough to charge him, unless the priest fingers him," Greene said. "But we can hold him overnight as a material witness. Maybe by morning we'll be able to interview Father Costello, get this whole thing settled."

"Maybe, but I wouldn't bet a lunch on it."

"How come?" Greene asked, arching an eyebrow.

Hafner squinted at his younger partner. "Look at it this way. If you were Father Costello, and you had this big urge to rehab ex-cons, would you finger one of your own guys? Or would you play dumb, try to handle the whole thing in-house?"

"You really think he'll refuse to cooperate with a police investigation?"

"Let's just say he could come down with a serious case of selective memory. Of course, that's providing he wakes up at all."

CHAPTER 6

Father Joe did wake up.

It happened in stages beginning early the next morning, Friday. At first, he was in and out. A nurse came into the Intensive Care Unit at five A.M. to do her rounds and heard him talking in his sleep. Around seven, his eyes came open for a few minutes. He was able to ask for water, ask where he was, before slipping back into sleep.

By nine, only twelve hours after the attack in the alley, Father Joe was out from under the effects of the painkillers and was talking clearly. But not clearly enough for the two detectives from Metro's Physical Crimes Unit.

"Look, Father," Greene said, keeping it low-key, "you've had a bad time. Maybe if you get a few more hours rest, things will make more sense to you."

"I feel fine, considering." The priest tried to raise himself higher, but the doctor who'd been treating him quickly objected to that idea.

"You must lie still on your back, Father. You've suffered a severe concussion." Doctor Halliday looked with disapproval from Father Joe to the sergeants. "He's had a severe concussion, I told you that."

"Three times," Hafner said, straight-faced.

The doctor, a serious young man with thinning hair, had no trouble returning the deadpan look. "We'll need to observe him for another twenty-four hours. He needs to rest and to lie still, gentlemen. You're lucky I've allowed you to speak with him at all."

"Yeah," Hafner said. "It's our lucky day."

"We'll keep it short, doctor," Greene said. "We just need to know what he saw."

"I've told you," Father Joe said as the doctor left the room. "I didn't really see anything. I guess I was daydreaming or something. Anyway, all I remember is somebody coming at me from the shadows. He grabbed me, I shouted out, then I guess he hit me." A small shrug. "The lights went out."

"Uh huh." Hafner glanced at Greene as if to say, I told you so. "So you're telling us you can't ID the guy who attacked you."

"I'm sorry, sergeant, but that's the way it is."

Hafner once again took in the complete package. A thin, pasty Catholic priest lying flat on a bed. Head bandaged, eyes still a little glassy from the dope they'd pumped into him. A victim, not a perp. And yet Hafner felt like strangling him right then and there.

Instead, he exhaled heavily and went to look out the window. Rule number one: two groups you didn't play hardball with were clergy and politicians. Not in Riverton anyway. If ever there was a time and a place for his partner's touchy-feely approach, this was it.

"Okay, Father," Greene said. "Maybe we should bring *you* up to speed. Has anyone told you about Chet Tomzak?"

"Chet? No. What about him?"

In his best courtroom voice, Sergeant Greene laid out the events that had followed the attack in the alley. How Chet Tomzak was found over the injured priest, holding the money pouch, smelling of whiskey. How they had taken Tomzak down to Metro for questioning the night before. How Sister Matty had come along around midnight and talked them into releasing him to her.

Father Joe's eyes widened with every word. "Surely you don't think Chet attacked me."

"Well, we haven't charged him. But right now I'd say he's both our key witness and our number one suspect, Father. I mean, if you add up all the pieces—"

"That's crazy," the priest said, his face beginning to turn as red as his beard. "I don't care what pieces you add, I can tell you right now they don't add up. It wasn't Chet Tomzak."

"You mean you don't want to believe it could've been Tomzak?"

"No, I mean it *wasn't* Chet. I know that for a fact. It wasn't any of the men from the program."

"Now, just a damn minute." Hafner stepped back up to the bed, forgetting his own rule. "If you didn't see anybody attack you, how can you say it *wasn't* Tomzak? Or any of those other mugs from that hash joint of yours?"

"Well, I—" Father Joe paused and closed his eyes for a moment. When he reopened them, he said, "I'm starting to remember things. Bits and pieces, all kind of cloudy. But the man who attacked me was taller than Chet. Taller than any of the men who work at the restaurant. Any of the white men, certainly."

Greene leaned over the bed a bit farther. "This tall white guy, what was he wearing, Father? You remember?"

"No, not really. It didn't register."

"A tan raincoat, maybe?"

"Could've been, I suppose. I really couldn't say."

"Right," Hafner said evenly. "So all you know for sure is it wasn't one of your boys. And we're just supposed to buy that?"

"Yes, sergeant. It wasn't one of my boys. I guess it was just a mugger, waiting out in the alley for whoever happened by. Luckily, he was chased off before he could steal the money, so there was no real harm done. I don't even see that this is a police matter any longer, since I won't be filing a complaint—"

"Whoa now, Father," Greene said. "You're lying there with your head cracked open, and you say no real harm done? Anyway, we're a little past the complaint stage on this one. We've got a couple of felonies here. You don't expect us to just drop it."

"I'm sorry, gentlemen. I don't know what I expect." He rubbed at his eyes gently. "I guess I'm still a bit groggy."

Doctor Halliday took that moment to reenter the room and shoo away the two detectives. "You've had your fifteen minutes and then some. Come back tomorrow. This patient needs rest."

"Who doesn't?" Hafner said as he and Greene went out the door.

*   *   *

They followed the green floor stripe back to the elevators, Hafner muttering the whole way.

"Son of a bitch. Didn't I tell you, Kel? No offense to God intended, but that priest is lying through his friggin' teeth."

"Hey, I tend to agree with you for once, partner. The man's playing us for some reason. The question is, why?"

"He's protecting Tomzak or one of the other cons, that's why. Bad publicity like this could dry up the funding for that Mercy House—"

"The Hard Time Cafe," Greene corrected him.

"Yeah, whatever. That's something else that scalds my butt. It's like they're making a joke out of doing time. Well, it'll be a cold day in hell before they ever see me and the missus taking a meal in that dump."

Greene figured it would be a cold day in hell before Hafner took his wife to any restaurant that didn't have a drive-up window. He also figured it wouldn't be wise to point that out just then.

Elevator six opened in front of them and out stepped Sister Matthew. Hafner noted with approval her clothing today: a black skirt to mid-calf and a simple white cotton blouse under a long black overcoat. Not quite a habit, but close enough to get the idea across. Probably she was trying to blend in with all the old-fashioned nuns he'd seen walking the halls of St. Mary's Hospital.

"Good morning, sergeants. I understand the patient is awake and alert."

"Yeah, he's bright as a new penny," Hafner said. "Telling stories even."

She looked up at him with that same icy glare she'd used the night before. Hafner could feel the sting of the ruler glinting out of those hazel eyes of hers.

Turning to Greene, she said, "Maybe you'd like to translate for your partner."

"Well, Sister, it's like this. We think the good Father is being less than honest with us about what he remembers or doesn't remember."

Greene went on to outline their interview with Father Joe. When he finished, he could see that she was as confused as they were about the priest's selective memory. Not that she was about to admit it.

"It's simple enough, gentleman. Father Joe's had a bad hit on the head. I'm sure all he needs is some extra rest." She glanced at Hafner. "And perhaps a friendly face to look at."

Hafner waited until she was down the hall and out of earshot before saying, "Well, one out of two ain't bad."

*   *   *

While Sister Matty had her short visit with Father Joe, several of the men waited impatiently in the hospital's lobby. Reuben Macky, Billboard, Ernie Pintaro, and Donzell Jepson had been refused visitors passes by the old biddy at the front desk. Special permission was needed to visit patients in the ICU, they were told.

And so they waited, huddled together in a corner near the elevators. Chet Tomzak had come along too. He sat in a green vinyl chair near the front window, a magazine on his lap, watching the rain come down outside. He felt exactly like a man in solitary, kept out of the general prison population for his own good.

On the ride over to St. Mary's that morning in the church van, the other men's silence had told him all he needed to know. Then one of them, Ernie Pintaro, an ex-pug, had caught his eye and said, "I don't know if you did it, man, but if you did, you're history."

Sister Matty had spoken up for him at that point. But she was the only one.

"Look at him over there," Billboard sneered now. "Reading a freakin' magazine like he's waitin' for a plane or somethin'."

"Give it a rest, man," Macky said quietly.

If anyone should have it in for Tomzak, it should be him. After all, it was his job that got split up to make room for the new man. Macky had gone from Manager to Operations Manager, with Tomzak taking on the role of Business Manager. The man didn't even have to work his way up, like Macky had done for three years.

Still, Macky knew it had been the right move, bringing in Tomzak. The dude had experience running a tavern and had a college degree in business. Truth be known, Macky was relieved when Sister Matty and Father Joe first came to him with the idea. None of them were that comfortable handling payroll and budget for the restaurant.

Macky hoped they hadn't all made a big mistake.

"Damn," Donzell said, "I hate this waitin' around."

"You oughta be used to it," Macky said. "You're a waiter, aren't you?"

"Oh, that's weak, man." Donzell jerked his head toward the window. "I'd go outside for a smoke, only I'd probably drown my ass."

"Matty won't be up there much longer. She knows we gotta get back, get ready to open the restaurant."

As if on cue, the elevator opened behind them and out came the Sister. The men immediately circled around her, but she put off their questions. She led them over to where Chester was waiting in the lounge area and sat them down.

"Well," she said, "Father Joe is doing very well. He should be home in a day or two good as new, the doctor tells me. But as far as the attack last night—he doesn't seem to remember very much about it."

Again the men all began talking at once, and again Sister Matty waved them off. When quiet was restored, she told them what little Father Joe had told her. However, she didn't tell them about her chance meeting with Sergeants Hafner and Greene.

"You know what bugs me the most?" Macky asked when Matty finished. "It's what Joe was doing in the first place, taking all that cash and heading out into the night like that. I mean, that's not how we usually do it."

"Usually we don't have that kind of bread," Billboard said. "Had to be, what? Two or three grand in that sack after all the business we did yesterday?"

Naturally they all looked to the business manager for a count.

Tomzak cleared his throat. "Just under three thousand." He nodded in Macky's direction. "Reuben and I took turns checking the till during the day. Whenever we got too much cash in there—anything over five hundred in small bills— we'd put the extra in the lockbox in the storage room."

Sister Matty shrugged. "As I said, Father Joe told me he was worried about keeping so much money in the lockbox. So he decided to take most of it over to the safe in the rectory."

"Yeah, but alone?" Macky asked. "Why didn't he ask one of us to go with him?"

"Maybe he did," Billboard said, staring darts at Tomzak.

Tomzak kept his cool, if barely. "He didn't say a word to me about taking any cash over to the rectory. I told you how it went down."

"Oh, yeah," Billboard said, smirking. "This tall geek in the raincoat who had an argument with Joe and then pounded him over the head. Except Matty says Joe don't remember any tall guy in a raincoat."

"He also said it wasn't Chester," the Sister cut in. "That much he remembered for certain."

"Unless he's just covering this guy's butt."

"Y'know, Billboard, you remind me of those two detectives," Tomzak said. "Only you're dumber and uglier."

Billboard cursed and started to get up, but Macky's beefy forearm pushed him back down. "Save your energy, hillbilly. You got a lotta cooking to do today." To Tomzak he said, "The thing is, if it really was this tall dude who went after Joe. And if you really saw Joe and the tall dude together in the alley earlier in the day—"

He let the thought drop, but everyone could see where he'd been headed. To believe Tomzak's version of events, you had to believe Father Joe was lying for some reason. But no one wanted to say it, not even Chet Tomzak.

But Tomzak knew what he had seen out there in that alley. Now all he had to do was convince everybody else. And he could think of only one way to do that.

Find the tall guy in the shabby tan raincoat.

CHAPTER 7

*His first impulse was to run.
To run like a son of a bitch and not stop until he saw palm
trees. But he was getting too old to hop freighters, and bus
tickets cost money.*

*He reached into his pocket, jangled the change, and felt
the thin roll of small bills he had left.*

Damn it! If only he'd gotten his money . . .

*For that was how he thought of it—his money. The priest
owed it to him. Hell, the world owed it to him, the kind of
hard luck he'd had all his life. And it had been right there,
in that sweet, fat money pouch. Oh, baby, just seeing that
wad had got him thinking, thinking why waste time with
another five hundred? Go for a grand, man. You'd live like
a king for two months on that kind of scratch.*

*Only Costello wasn't going for it. Didn't even wanna
fork over the five bills, let alone an extra five. Priest tried*

to talk him out of his money, tried to make him see "the error of his ways."

That's when he'd lost it. He didn't mean to hit him that hard, not the second time, but it wasn't his fault. Joe should've known not to try pushing him around. Son of a bitch didn't give him any choice, talking back to him like that.

But, Jesus, he'd hit Costello too hard. And then that other prick came out of nowhere, and suddenly there was nothing to do but run.

And that's what he knew he should do now. Go south. Hop a freight train if he had to, but get going. Fear was a great motivator, always had been in his life. But not as great as greed. And that's why, instead of running, he sat in his room and told himself all the reasons he should stick around.

First, there was the money. Plenty of it, and plenty more to come, judging by the crowd he'd seen at that restaurant Costello was running for the cons. A thousand bucks from the till every once in a while—say once a month—wouldn't even be missed. And, hey, he's an ex-con himself, right? So it was almost like they owed it to him.

Anyway, it was Father Joe's operation, wasn't it? He could make an extra grand disappear from the books without breaking a sweat.

That was the other thing: the priest. Maybe he'd learned his lesson, huh? No more trying to weasel out of paying the money, because he knows what that would get him. And Costello wouldn't talk, either. He was sure of that. Old Joe had had plenty of chances to go to the cops before and he didn't. And he wouldn't now.

So he was safe on that score. Nobody was looking for him.

Or so he thought.

*   *   *

"Another ginger ale, buddy?"

Tomzak ignored the bartender's smirk. "No, thanks. I'm good."

"Driving, huh?"

"Something like that."

"Right." He gave out a humorless chuckle and moved farther down the bar.

Tomzak knew what the bartender was thinking. It was the same thing Tomzak would think if a stranger came into the place he used to manage and spent an hour drinking ginger ale and asking questions about a tall man in a raincoat.

Undercover cop. That's what the bartender had him pegged as. If Tomzak wasn't so square looking, it'd be different. If he looked like Billboard, the guy would figure it was a heist or a drug deal in the making.

But Chet Tomzak was a walking loaf of Wonder Bread, through and through. He'd learned that in the yard at Calderwood. It may have been medium security, not maximum like Arcadia where most of the ex-cons at the cafe had done time. It may have had chain link and razor wire strung around the perimeter instead of a twenty-foot wall. But it was still a prison. And the men inside that wire were still hard men. They had a look and a manner about them that Tomzak hadn't picked up even with four years inside.

So in the mind of the bartender and probably everyone else in the place, he had to be a cop working undercover. And that was okay. He'd been able to use that to his advantage.

The Ace Lounge was the name of the place. It was the second bar he'd hit since coming off work at 9:30. It was now a little after 11:00, still early for a Friday night in any of the city's eastside juke joints. But it felt much later to Tomzak. It had been a long day.

Business at The Hard Time Cafe hadn't slacked off very much from yesterday's grand opening. The hungry and the curious began pouring in at 11:30 for lunch. The dinner crowd was even bigger. By eight o'clock they were turning people away at the door. And at 9:30, half an hour past official closing, there still had been a dozen customers finishing their dinners.

They were a hit, Tomzak thought bitterly. Too bad nobody was enjoying it.

Everyone had done their job and done it well. But there was a cloud hanging over the place the entire day. Father Joe was not there to give out a pat on the back or a word of encouragement. The men's anger and resentment were deeply felt by Tomzak.

Which is why he had to find the mystery man, the tall man in the shabby tan raincoat. He had to find out who the guy was and point the police in his direction. Then Tomzak could get the heat off him. Or maybe he wouldn't leave it to the cops. They didn't believe him anyway. Maybe he'd just face the guy himself, find out what it is he had on Father Joe.

It had to be blackmail or something like that. Otherwise, why was Father Joe pretending he didn't remember who hit him? And he was pretending, that much Tomzak was sure of.

He'd tried explaining it to Macky that morning. With Tomzak himself following Father Joe in the alley, that meant the tall guy had to have attacked him from head-on. Joe had to see him coming because there was no place to hide in the well-lit alley.

But all Macky had said was, "That makes sense, man. *If* there was a tall guy in the first place. Otherwise, it could be Joe's just covering your ass."

"You believe that, Reuben? That I could do that—?"

Macky had stared at him for a long time before he answered. "No, I don't believe that. But some around here do. And they're gonna keep on believing it until they find out different."

Tomzak sipped the ginger ale and made a face. The sweetness of the soft drink was getting to him, lying on his stomach like syrup. But he'd make do with it, no problem. That was one promise to himself he intended to keep: no more booze, ever.

This was the first time he'd been in a bar since that deadly night five years back. If he had a choice he wouldn't be in one now, let alone bar hopping from place to place. His reasoning was simple enough. The guy who attacked Father Joe wore shabby clothes and traveled with a pint of whiskey in his pocket. That told Tomzak the tall man was a boozer—a down-and-outer who for some reason had his hooks into the priest.

But his reasoning had led him one step further. The pint the guy was carrying—the one he'd slugged Joe with—wasn't some off-the-shelf rotgut. It was Jim Beam. That had to mean the tall man was reasonably flush, spending money on the good stuff. Maybe he'd already hit up Father Joe for money once and was coming back for more last night. Only things had gone bad, he didn't get his money, and he'd left a priest bleeding on the pavement.

The odds said that the tall man had already headed out of town or at least gone underground. That's what anybody with common sense would do, get as far away from the scene of the crime as quickly as he could. If the tall man *had* run, then Tomzak was screwed. No way to get himself off the hook with the police or, more importantly in his mind, with the guys at The Hard Time Cafe.

But Tomzak was gambling that the tall man hadn't run. Like a lot of life's low-end losers, this guy was lazy and a creature of habit. If he thought there was still a score to be made, he'd convince himself to stick around. He'd think he was too smart to get caught. Tomzak had met a lot of guys like that in his four years in prison. He had to hope the tall man was just like all the others.

So he asked himself, a guy like that, where's he likely to spend his nights in this neighborhood? In one of the neighborhood taverns. But not the upscale fern bars found farther up Carson Avenue, toward midtown. No, buying Jim Beam was one thing, but our man wouldn't be the type who'd pay extra for cut crystal or a fancy coaster under the glass. Our guy was a maintenance drinker, pure and simple.

So check out the working-class taverns along eastern Carson Avenue and its side streets. Places like Ron's Oasis, which Tomzak had visited first with no luck, and now The Ace Lounge.

He checked the Budweiser clock behind the bar again, then gave the patrons another glance. There were only half a dozen in the place and he'd already spoken to all of them. He pushed away the glass of ginger ale and started to get up, thinking he'd move on to the next joint. But as he did so, the door swung open and into the bar came a round little man wearing a Chicago Cubs baseball cap.

Tomzak waited for him to settle on a stool, waited for the bartender to bring the little man a beer, heard the bartender call him by name: Trippy. Then, taking his drink with him, Tomzak moved down the bar and leaned in next to the guy.

"A Cubs fan, huh?" Tomzak said, knowing how lame an opener it was even as the words came out of his mouth. The little guy thought so too.

"Or maybe I just found the hat, ever think of that? Just something to keep the dew off the old melon."

Tomzak decided to go in another direction.

"Trippy," he said. "That's some kind of nickname, right?"

The little man took him in with a frown, then went back to sipping the head off his beer. After a moment, he said, "Not that it's anyone's business, fella, but it's my last name. Trippi, with an *i*. It's Italian."

"You don't look Italian."

"Yeah? Well, you don't look like a fag, either. I guess you never can tell." He chuckled into his glass and gave a wink to the bartender.

On balance, Tomzak liked it better when they were mistaking him for a cop. "Very funny. You're a real card, Trippi. Look, the thing is, I'm looking for a man—"

"I rest my case," Trippi said to the bartender, and they both laughed.

"—a tall man, broad in the shoulders. Wears an old tan raincoat. Likes Jim Beam when he can get it." Tomzak waited for a response. When none came, he added, "It's important I find this guy."

"Not to me."

Tomzak sighed. He was tired and discouraged to begin with. Now he had to put up with a fearless, frustrating little man in a baseball cap. Probably a waste of time anyway. No one else in the place had been any help, and there was no reason to think this clown would be, either.

He thought about leaving, then stopped himself. If Chet Tomzak had anything going for him, it was that he was thorough and methodical. Take care of the details, make sure to dot all the *i*'s and cross all the *t*'s, and things would work out. It's what had made him a good manager, and it's what now made him stay.

"Look," he said. "This guy I'm looking for may have attacked a priest last night."

That took the satisfied grin off Trippi's face. "You mean Father Joe, over to Corpus Christi?"

"Yeah, that's right."

"Why didn't you say so? Tall guy in a raincoat, you said? His name wouldn't be Carl by any chance?"

Tomzak sat on a stool next to the little man. "You tell me."

Trippi shrugged. "I don't know if it's the same guy, but I run into this fella over at O'Mara's, over on Braun Street? Kitty-corner from Corpus Christi, now I think about it. Anyway, he said his name was Carl. I didn't get a last name, so don't ask."

"But he was tall, broad-shouldered?"

"Yeah, yeah. Kinda reddish hair, curly and going bald. I should talk." He took off the Cubs cap, revealing a hairless pink dome of skin. "Come to think of it, it's this baseball cap got the guy talking to me in the first place. He said he grew up in Chicago, been a Cubs fan all his life."

CHAPTER
8

Sergeant Hafner held the jelly donut out in front of him and took a small bite. Didn't help. He still got a sprinkle of powdered sugar on his pants and a glob of raspberry jam oozing out the back.

"Damn." He licked away the raspberry glob just before it could drop off and land on his shoes. Around bites of the donut he said, "Remind me to go with the glazed next time."

"Go with the glazed next time."

"Thanks. I got two teenagers at home and a wife going through the change. What I really need is a wise-ass partner."

Sergeant Greene polished off the last of his blueberry bran muffin. He blew on his fingers to ward off the March chill. "You drag me out here at nine on a Saturday morning, you're lucky sass is all I give you."

"Out here" was the side parking lot of The Donut Hole on Carson Avenue, about four blocks east of Corpus Christi Church. The location was not a coincidence.

"You know," Greene said as he tossed his napkin into the dumpster beside their car, "it wouldn't hurt to back off a little on this thing. I mean, with the caseload we've got, to be putting in OT on an assault where the victim doesn't even want to press charges—"

Hafner gave him a look. "It's not the overtime that's bugging you, it's Tomzak. You think we're chasing the wrong dog."

Greene opened the driver's door and slid in behind the wheel of the vanilla Ford. He waited until Hafner finished his donut and climbed into the passenger seat before laying out his answer.

"What I think is you need to put this case in perspective, Harold. It's one thing to hammer a perp, or even to come down hard on a suspect. But this time—" he paused, searching for the right words. "You're as angry at the victim as you are at the crime. I mean, everything about this case seems to piss you off."

"That's what you think, huh?"

"Yeah, I do. And I think it's messing up your objectivity."

"Objectivity." Hafner snorted.

"Go ahead, laugh it off. We both know I'm right. You got a burr up your butt on this for some reason and it's screwing up your judgment."

Hafner half-turned in his seat. "It is *not* screwing up my judgment. I *told* you why we needed to be out here, and you agreed it was as good as anything else we've got. So spare me the Sociology 101 crap and just drive, okay?"

Without a word, Greene backed the Ford from its slot, then eased the car out onto Carson Avenue, heading east.

The silence between the two men stretched for three blocks. Finally, Hafner, staring straight ahead, broke the ice.

"I went to Catholic school for a while, I ever tell you that?"

"No." Greene looked over. "I thought you were Lutheran."

"I am, born and raised."

"But not born again."

Hafner chuckled. "No, we don't do that. Anyway, I was going into the seventh grade at Franklin Junior High, the old one over on the west side. I grew up over that way, right off Lowell Avenue."

Greene did know that much about his partner's youth, but he let him keep talking.

"So I'm about to leave the neighborhood elementary school, right? And my mother's all upset because, let's face it, even back in the Sixties, Franklin didn't have what you'd call a good reputation."

"What, too many of the 'wrong element' moving into the neighborhood?"

"C'mon, Kel, don't start playing the race card with me. We've been down too many alleys together."

"You got a point." Greene moved into the left lane and signaled a turn at Halstead Street. Just down the block was a rooming house where several of Father Costello's ex-cons lived, including Chet Tomzak. "So you went to Catholic school?"

"Just for that one year. Then we ended up moving to suburbia along with about half the old neighborhood, seems like."

"They call it 'white flight'."

"Yeah, well, whatever. My point is that one year at St. Monica's was like a trip to hell. White shirt, stupid-ass red tie, black slacks you could bag groceries in. Religion classes every day with old Father Wozniak. But the worst was the nuns."

"Pretty strict, huh?"

"Strict? Jesus. We had this one old bat, Sister Immaculata. Big Mac we called her, and this was before there was a McDonald's on every corner. Big Mac taught geography, always had this long wooden pointer in her hand to point out places on the map, right? Only what she really used it for was to whack anyone who nodded off or screwed up an assignment. I mean, this old broad had a swing Tony Gwynn would envy."

"A contact hitter."

"Never missed." Hafner shook his head. "Man, every time I'm around priests or nuns I get flashbacks. I guess that makes me sort of defensive."

"Mmm." Greene found a parking spot near the boardinghouse and pulled over. "So we're here to hassle Tomzak and some of his ex-con buddies because you've got an anti-Catholic bias, is that about it?"

"No, I got no anti-Catholic anything. I just get a little hyper sometimes around certain types of clergy." Hafner shoved open his door. "Anyway, I already told you. What we're here for is to beat the bushes a little, then watch to see which way the rabbit runs."

*   *   *

"Why me?" Sister Matty wanted to know.

For once, she wasn't kneeling in a front-left pew at Corpus Christi, having just lit a votive candle, when she asked the question. And for once, she got a clear-cut answer.

"Because you got a better look at the guy than I did. You saw him indoors, under good lighting. I just caught a side view in an alley and then the back of his head when he ran away."

"Oh, Chester." She chewed on her lower lip as she thought about it. "I'm a nun, for pity's sake. I can't hang around in a tavern waiting for this man to appear. What would people think?"

"The hell with people." Tomzak dipped his head. "I'm sorry, Sister. I understand what you're saying, but this is very important to me. Look, couldn't you wear a disguise or something? I mean, it's not like you wear a habit anyway, so who's to know?"

"Timothy O'Mara, for one. He owns that place, in addition to being one of our parishioners here at Corpus Christi. He'd recognize me in a heartbeat. Anyway, Father Joe's coming home from the hospital today. I really should go along to pick him up."

"Reuben can pick him up by himself."

They were talking in the south apse, a tall rounded area that served as the main entrance hall for the church. Sister Matty sat on a side bench while the high-strung Chester Tomzak paced. Even though they spoke quietly, their words echoed off the marble floor and the high domed ceiling.

"Besides, Chester, we don't even know if this Carl is the same man, or if he'll even show up again."

"He will! I'm sure of it."

But he didn't look sure, Sister Matty thought. Merely desperate.

"If there were some stronger connection," she said. "Did the little man in the baseball cap tell you anything else, other than the man's name is Carl and he's losing his hair?"

Tomzak stopped pacing, frowned as he thought about it. "Did I mention the guy's from Chicago?"

"Chicago?" The sister straightened. "He grew up in Chicago? Are you sure?"

"That's what Trippi told me. It's what got the tall guy talking to him in the first place, that Cubs cap Trippi wears. Why, does that mean something?"

"Father Joe is from Chicago. The north side where all the Cubs fans are."

"Hah! See, I knew there was a connection."

"Oh, my. I'm starting to agree with you, Chester, and I'm not at all happy about it."

"Why not? This could get me off the hook. If I can prove this guy was blackmailing Father Joe, prove they knew each other from the old days—"

Sister Matty was shaking her head sadly. "But it would also prove Father Joe lied to the police. And to me. It would take some terrible burden to make him do that, and that's why I'm unhappy at the prospect."

"To save myself, I may have to hurt Father Joe," Tomzak said, turning away. "Forget I asked, Sister. I wouldn't want to put you in that position. I'm not even sure I want to put myself in that position. Maybe I should just take the heat—"

"No, Chester, I didn't mean it that way. If we stop looking for the truth, we're all lost." She let go a rattling sigh. "I'll go along with you. But first I want you to come with me."

"Where to?" he asked as she rose from the bench and headed into the church proper.

She looked back at him with a Mona Lisa smile. "How better to start a search than by lighting a candle, eh?"

*   *   *

"This is ridiculous." She tugged down on the bill of her cap again and nudged the dark glasses back up the bridge of her nose. "Wearing sunglasses indoors only makes a person stand out more."

Tomzak shrugged. "It was your idea."

"I beg your pardon. You're the one who suggested I wear a disguise."

"I meant like a wig or something."

"I didn't have a wig handy, did I? Believe it or not, Chester, wigs aren't standard issue in my order."

It was nearly noon and they were in a side booth at O'Mara's. They'd been there over two hours, nursing soft drinks and munching pretzels. The tavern was beginning to fill up with the lunch trade, but the man named Carl hadn't put in an appearance.

"Are you sure they can cover for you at the restaurant this afternoon?" Matty asked for the third time.

"It's a Saturday," Tomzak said. "We'll be lucky to get a quarter of the crowd we had during the week. All the midtown business people are home in their safe suburbs today, you know that. And I went in first thing this morning to handle a few things."

"Still, you don't want to give the other men any more reason to be upset with you. Maybe we should head back—"

He reached across the table, put his hand on her forearm. "They're already as mad as they're going to get. The only way I can change that is to come back with proof that this Carl character is real. *Please*, Matty."

"All right, Chester. We'll give it the rest of the afternoon. But if this man doesn't turn up, I say we go directly to Father Joe with what—"

"Sister Matthew? Is that you under there?"

She shot a glance up at the woman approaching the booth, said, "Oh, my," and turned her face toward the wall.

"That is you, isn't it? C'mon, Sister, the Lord's already seen you. There's no sense hiding from the rest of us."

Matty slowly turned around again, removing the sunglasses as she did so. With a small grin she said, "Hello, Helen. I thought you worked nights."

"I do. In fact, that's why I was coming over to your booth to see this fella. We spoke last night about your mystery man."

She was a large woman with a rosy glow, orange hair, and a split between her two front teeth. Helen O'Mara Boyle, sister to the tavern's owner and a barmaid of long standing. Also a long-standing member of the Corpus Christi parish. And better than the Sunday notice at spreading information. By Monday, half the women in the Holy Name Society would know Sister Matthew had been spotted sharing a booth with a man at O'Mara's.

Matty decided she'd better try to salvage what she could of the situation. She pulled the big woman down beside her in the booth and, in a low voice, said, "Chester thinks the man who attacked Father Joe is a patron of yours, Helen. He's brought me in to ID the fellow."

"I figured as much," Helen said in as close to a whisper as she could manage. "That's why I came over." To Tomzak she said, "After you came by last night? It wasn't half an hour later that this Carl came in again."

Tomzak leaned across the table eagerly. "Did you talk to him? Were you able to find out anything more about him?"

"No, I'm afraid not. He wasn't in a talking mood. He had just the one glass of whiskey and left. There was one thing, though—"

"Yeah?"

"Well, I noticed he paid with a dollar bill and a handful of change." Her ruby lips turned downward. "You see that a lot, some poor panhandler comes in and pays out every last cent for a drink. An alkie like that, I wouldn't even serve 'em, but you know they'd just go down the block to Four Kings or Arena's."

Tomzak said to Matty, "He's broke again. If I'm right, that could mean he'll make another move on Father Joe. If we can find him first, make him talk—"

"I'm not sure I like the sound of that, Chester."

"I don't mean get rough. If he's hurting, we might get his story for a bottle or even a hot meal—"

"That's the other thing I was going to tell you," Helen cut in. "He looked awfully hungry to me. So I did what I always do when we get someone like that in here. I gave him one of those cards Father Joe leaves off, the ones with the information on The Loaves and Fishes. Told him he could get himself a good meal for free with no preaching."

Tomzak laughed harshly. "You told him to go to Corpus Christi's soup kitchen? What'd he say to that?"

"Well, he just stared at the card for a minute. Then he kind of chuckled and said, 'Why the hell not?'"

CHAPTER 9

While Sister Matty and Chet Tomzak were out at O'Mara's, Father Joe Costello was returning to the rectory and his second-floor office. He usually enjoyed the silence there; it was his sanctuary. But today the room seemed to be filled with threatening shadows and trouble. Perhaps that's why, as soon as the telephone on his old cherry desk rang, he knew who it was.

"Hello?"

"Hello, Joey. I'm glad you're back. Listen, I'm sorry about the other night, but I warned you. You know all about this goddamn temper of mine. It's been getting me in trouble since we were kids. Hey, you remember the time we chucked rocks at the Polack punks down on—"

"You didn't call to chat about the old days, Carl," Father Joe cut him off. "And I'm not interested if you did."

"Yeah, well, course not. You'd like to forget all about your misspent youth, huh, Joey." What began as a laugh turned into a coughing fit.

"Sounds like you're still taking care of yourself."

"That's the thing, Joey. This shitty weather up here's killing me. Rent's coming due on my room. I haven't had a decent meal in two days. A man can't take care of himself without money now, can he?"

"If you'd spend the money on food instead of whiskey—"

"I don't need a lecture!"

"You're drunk now, aren't you? I can hear the slur in your words."

"Hah! I'm down to half a pint of Four Roses, hardly enough to put a cat to sleep. I'll be fine, don't worry about that. All I need from you, Joey, is my money."

"Carl, think what you're doing—"

"Shut it, priest! No more preaching," he hissed. "Think about what happened the last time you tried to preach to me. And think about this: you might not wanna chat about the old days but I do, and there's plenty of people who'd be interested in what I got to say."

Father Joe started to reply, then caught himself. He forced himself to think, but not about Carl's threats. Instead, he thought about his options now that he had some. Finally he said, "Things have changed, Carl. You assaulted me, remember? If I identify you to the police, you're going back to jail for a good long time."

"You can't turn me in without hurting yourself, Costello."

"And you can't expose me without putting yourself at risk," Father Joe said, struggling to remain calm. "It's a stalemate."

Now it was Carl's turn to lapse into a thoughtful

silence. Presently he said, "You want me gone for good, right, Joey? Well, my friend, that takes traveling money."

"How do I know you'll really go this time? You said last time—"

"Last time I had the upper hand. Like you said, we're in a stalemate now." He hacked out a bitter cough. "Besides, my blood's got too thin for the North. I'll be moving on."

Father Joe wanted to believe him. It made him sick at the pit of his stomach to give this man money, to buy his silence. But if he didn't, he would lose everything. He couldn't risk that, not with all the work he had to do.

He sighed his surrender. "I won't have much cash on hand until this evening after the restaurant closes."

*   *   *

The Loaves and Fishes opened every day at two in the afternoon and closed at nine. The hours had been decided by experience. Open any earlier and the flow of street people into the place was too slight to keep the volunteer servers and cooks busy. Stay open any later and there wouldn't be any volunteers, since they all had homes and lives to get back to.

The card Helen had given to the man called Carl gave both the address and the operating hours for Corpus Christi's free food kitchen. That's how Sister Matty and Chet Tomzak knew they had a couple of hours to spare before continuing their search at The Loaves and Fishes. If their mystery man was going to show up for a meal, he couldn't do it before two o'clock.

In the meantime, Tomzak hurried back to The Hard Time Cafe to put in some time on the job. Sister Matty decided to return to the rectory to welcome Father Joe back to his flock and perhaps to coax a few answers from him.

She found him in his office. He was seated at his big old desk, his fingers steepled, lost in thought. The large window behind him looked out over Braun Street. O'Mara's Tavern was just across the way, down half a block Matty realized. And she wondered, *Did that awful man choose O'Mara's just so he could keep tabs on Father Joe?*

"Oh, hello, Sister Matthew."

He was still wearing a bandage on the left side of his skull where he'd had the stitches. He was still looking as distracted as he had for weeks before the attack. Sister Matty didn't know what to do. Half of her wanted to reach out to him, to give comfort. The other half wanted to take him by the shoulders and give him a good shake.

"It's good to have you back, Father," is all she managed.

"It's good to be back." He smiled weakly. "Well, they say a conservative is just a liberal who's been mugged. Now's my chance to prove them wrong." He sat up straight and patted a folder on the desk. "Long as you're here, Sister, we may as well get something done. Shall we review next month's agenda?"

Sister Matty took the side chair and they set to work. More than an hour flew by as they went over the April calendar. There were meetings with trustees of the church, fund-drive events, parole board hearings to attend, not to forget daily masses and all the outreach programs to oversee. It was a workload that would tax any five people, but Father Joe and Sister Matty never complained.

The little wooden sign on Father Joe's desk said all there was to say on the subject: *Do all you can, then do some more.*

When they had finished, it was almost two o'clock. The tea and sandwiches Mrs. Clooney, the housekeeper, had brought up were reduced to two empty cups and a few crumbs on the serving plate. Sister Matty checked the mantel clock. She was eager get over to The Loaves and Fishes. But first she wanted to try and convince Father Joe to open up to her about his troubles, for it was plain as the beard on his face that he was deeply bothered by something. It had to be the tall man.

"Father," she said at last. "I was talking with Chester earlier. About this man he and I both saw hanging around the restaurant recently. The one who may've attacked you?"

He arched an eyebrow. "Yes, Matty?"

"Well, you see, we've asked around a bit for a man fitting that description. And, well, there is this person named Carl—"

Father Costello shot forward in his chair. "You've asked around a bit? That's what you've been doing while I was laid up—playing detective? It's no wonder we're falling farther behind in all our outreach programs, Sister."

She was taken aback. "That's hardly fair. We were gone only a few hours."

"A few hours that could've gone to some of this paperwork, or to calling round to our donors for more food and clothing. Or a dozen other things that need doing, not chasing after a phantom."

"This man is not a phantom, Father, and I think you know that."

"What I know, Sister, is that this whole business is no concern of yours. I want you to drop it. For God's sake, *I'm* the victim, remember? And if I don't want the matter pursued, that should be enough."

His face was red as a cardinal's cape. Given his recent trauma, Sister Matty was worried that this outburst might be enough to land him right back in the hospital. She did her best to control her own anger, to lower the tone of the conversation, but she simply couldn't leave without making her point.

"Yes, Father, you're the victim here, but not the only one. Chester Tomzak is also a victim. Not only is he the subject of a police investigation, but the other men are all down on him."

"But that's crazy. I cleared Chet with the police, and I've told you and Reuben the same thing. Chet wasn't the one—"

She held up her palm like a traffic cop. "I know you've told everyone, and so have I. But some of the men don't believe it. They already resented Chester for being different from them. Now they choose to believe that you're covering up for him."

"Well, that's just asinine. I'm sorry, but I've done all I can do on the subject. If some of the men are holding childish grudges, they're just going to have get over it." He shook his head, then thought better of it and lightly touched his bandage. "You know, Sister, Chet could take a lot of the pressure off himself if he'd just talk to the other men. Let them know who he is, where he came from, what he did."

"I agree, but we both know he can't do it. Not yet. The guilt he feels is still too strong, even after all these years."

"Yes, after all these years." Father Costello fell back into the depths of his chair and was silent for a few heartbeats. Then quietly he said, "Well, perhaps guilt has its place in God's plan too, or else why give man a conscience? Maybe a man *shouldn't* be able to put all his sins behind him. Maybe memory is His way of making us do penance."

He was still talking as he turned to look out the window, but Sister Matty realized he was talking to himself, not to her. She rose quietly and left the room.

CHAPTER
10

The office at The Hard Time Cafe was nothing like Father Joe's big office. In truth, it was a converted walk-in storage closet, just large enough to hold a battered rolltop desk, a chair, and a file cabinet. It also had no door, prompting Donzell Jepson to knock on the door jamb.

Chet Tomzak looked up from the desk. "Yeah, Donzell?"

"Telephone, man."

The restaurant's only phone was up at the front counter. Tomzak closed the account book and put it back in the desk. "Okay, thanks."

He walked up the short hallway that led past the restrooms and out across the dining room. "Huntsville," a prison song by Merle Haggard, was playing on the tape loop. It was half past two and the room was nearly empty. But the lunch crowd had been bigger than normal for a Saturday, and a fair amount of reservations had come in for dinner. The place was going to do just fine, Tomzak decided as he picked up the phone.

"It's me," said a breathless Sister Matty.

"Oh, hi. I got delayed here, but I'm on my way over to the food kitchen now—"

"Don't bother. Our man has been in already, and now he's back out on the street again."

"What? Already? Are you sure it's him, Matty?"

"It's him. He was there when I came down from the rectory, sitting by himself having a bologna sandwich and an apple. I almost went over and gave him a piece of my mind." She was still burning from her argument with Father Joe. "Anyway, I followed him as far as the street and then I grabbed a pay phone. He's heading your way, east on Carson."

"Probably he's living at one of the boardinghouses down this way," Tomzak said. "I'll go out and watch for him, see if I can follow him back to where he lives. Then I can pay a call later with a couple of the guys. See if we can't scare the story out of him."

Matty put on her schoolmarm voice. "Make certain that's all you boys do, Chester. No rough stuff. If he won't talk, we can always call in the police. Now I'd better run or I'll lose him."

"No, that's okay, Sister. I can take it from here."

"I just want to make sure he doesn't turn off someplace before he gets to you. I'll meet you across the street from the cafe, all right? Five minutes."

"Okay, but—" Before he could get in another word, the line went dead.

Tomzak started for the front door, then noticed the newspapers and candy wrappers blowing around out on

Carson Avenue. It was cold for late March, and that breeze would cool things down even more. He decided he had time to go back to the office for his jacket.

"Hold it, asshole."

Tomzak had just stepped out of the tiny office and was putting on his jacket when Billboard stepped into the hallway, blocking him from leaving.

"I have to go, man."

"Yeah, run off and let the rest of us do the work. You're good at that, Tomzak, runnin' away and leavin' a mess behind."

"I don't have time for this."

He tried to go around him, but Billboard pushed him back. He was wearing a white T-shirt under a chef's apron, exposing the ranks of crude tattoos that marched up both his arms.

"Those two cops came around today," he said. "They were lookin' to roust your sorry ass. Since you wasn't around, they decided to give me and some of the guys the business instead. We're gettin' sick of taking your heat, asshole."

Tomzak felt the blood rush into his face. "Look, I'm supposed to be meeting Sister Matty."

"Yeah? Well, you're meetin' with me now."

Tomzak knew Billboard was a professional brawler from way back, a guy who could kick the crap out of him without breaking a sweat. But he also knew that Matty was out on the street because of him. Waiting for him, depending on him. He couldn't let her down.

That's why he lowered his head and launched himself at Billboard like a cruise missile. He caught the taller man in the stomach, knocking him backward into the pea green wall, then tried another end run. He slipped past, thought he was in the clear. But Billboard's long fingers clamped onto the back of his jacket and wouldn't let go.

They tumbled out into the dining room, all fists and elbows, grunts and groans. The handful of patrons still in the restaurant sat frozen at their tables. In moments, the noise brought the waiters and the kitchen crew running.

"Hey! Hey! Hey!" Reuben Macky shouted the word over and over as he fought to separate the tangled men. After several seconds he succeeded, shoving Billboard into the hands of Donzell and Ernie and hanging onto Tomzak himself. With a glance at the wide-eyed customers, he said, "Let's take this out back, sort things out."

When Tomzak tried to talk, Macky told him to shut up until they were outside. He was half dragged, half shoved through the kitchen and out into the alley.

"Okay," Macky said, staring down Billboard. "What in the hell was that all about, like I couldn't guess."

Billboard swiped at a trickle of blood where Tomzak had managed to scratch his cheek. "Hey, don't look at me, man. I just wanted to talk to this punk, and he went apeshit on me."

"Right. You were just an innocent bystander."

"Jesus Christ!" Tomzak shrieked. "Will you stupid bastards shut the hell up and listen to me for once?"

*   *   *

Out on Carson Avenue, the wind was still gusting and the blue skies were turning steely. Sister Matty thought the windchill must be down near freezing. Not the sort of weather for a pair of Keds and a windbreaker. Yet there she was, standing on the corner opposite The Hard Time Cafe, shivering and shifting from foot to foot.

"Where *are* you, Chester," she murmured into her upturned collar.

She could see, nearly a block farther east along Carson, the retreating back of the tall man in the raincoat. In another minute he'd be gone.

She looked across at the cafe again. Then she said, "Oh, Lord, give me the strength." She turned to the east and walked as quickly as seemed wise. She covered the first block in half a minute, passing a pizza shop and a branch bank. She even hurried past Romano's Deli without her usual smile and wave to the people inside. Carl was still a block ahead of her.

She stopped at the cross street to let a few cars pass. As she scurried across against the light, she tried to focus on her target again. She almost panicked when she didn't pick him out right away, but then she saw a flash of the flapping tan raincoat as it disappeared around the next corner.

That corner, she realized, was Pierson Lane. Not much more than an alley, really. It connected Carson Avenue to Gregory Street, a narrow street of low-rent apartment buildings.

She hesitated when she reached the corner. Pierson Lane stretched ahead of her for some five hundred feet. Four-story buildings loomed on either side, trapping shadows along its length. There was a sidewalk along the right side of the lane, but several illegally parked cars and trucks had turned it into an obstacle course.

Sister Matty exhaled. *In for a penny . . .*

She picked her way down the sidewalk, around cars and over puddles. Other than acting as a shortcut to Gregory Street, Pierson Lane was there to provide access to the service entrances and the basements of buildings that fronted on Carson or Gregory.

It was from one such dark service door that a long arm shot out and pulled Sister Matty into its coil.

"Ahhpp—!" She swallowed a scream, in part because the arm was pushing so hard against her throat.

"Don't fight me, girly. If I wanted to, I could snap your neck like a stick."

She stopped struggling. He smelled of whiskey and stale tobacco and old sweat. The arm around her neck and the body pressing up against her felt like it was all bone and gristle. With a quickness she wouldn't have thought possible, he spun around in front of her, pushing her back hard against the green steel door.

"Now," he said, his voice as coarse as raw wool, "who the hell are you, and why'd you follow me?"

"I— I'm—" She was thrown off by the sudden closeness of the man and his homeliness. She stared up at his face, hanging a foot above her. It was as if one of the church's stone gargoyles had climbed down from the eaves to terrify her. "I'm Sister Matthew. I work with Father Costello."

"So where's your habit? Costello got you working plainclothes this week?"

"My order doesn't require us to wear the habit," she said calmly. She was beginning to feel her self-control returning. She hadn't been working with ex-cons for ten years only to turn to mush when some tough guy tried to scare her. "Your name is Carl, I believe."

"Believe what you like, girly."

"Why have you been harassing Father Costello?"

He laughed, a sound like coal thundering down a chute. "Is that what he calls it, harassment? We've got business, that's all. He owes me from way back."

"Do you always do business deals by smashing the other person's head with a whiskey bottle?"

The arm that had her pinned against the door now slid back up to Matty's throat. He came close, so close her eyes watered at the smell of his sour breath. His eyes were a liquid blue, bloodshot and faded.

"You don't ask questions, bitch, got that? You wanna dress like every other broad, I'll damn well treat you like one. In my day, a nun looked like a goddamn nun!"

Matty was barely able to breathe. She tried to pull his arm down off her throat, but he wouldn't budge. Nor did he seem to care that she was gasping for air. He was centered on his own rage; there was no room for anything else.

"You listening to me, girly? You tell Joey he'd better be there tonight, and no tricks. Everybody else paid for that killing and now it's his turn. I want my money, you hear me? I—want—my—money!"

With each of the last four words, he pushed a little harder against Matty's throat.

"You understand me, girly?"

"Yuhhnn—" She tried to form the word *yes*, but it wouldn't come out. And then everything started to go dim.

*   *   *

Chet Tomzak came out of Romano's Deli and stuffed his hands into his jacket. "This way," is all he said to Reuben Macky before turning east on Carson.

"They saw her?" Macky said, catching up.

"Yeah, they saw her. Five or ten minutes ago."

"We'll find her, man."

"We'd better," is all Tomzak would allow himself to say.

They came to the cross street and looked hopelessly in all four directions. Then they looked at each other and Macky shrugged. "Stay on the main drag, I'd say. See if any of the merchants on the next block saw her."

"We could split up."

"Yeah, but we already got guys out all over the neighborhood. We said we'd do out east on Carson."

Without a word, Tomzak trotted across the street with Macky following. They continued down Carson Avenue. Halfway down the block they checked with the woman at the dry cleaners, but she didn't remember seeing Sister Matty go by.

"She missed her, that's all," Macky said as they came out. "Woman's too busy reading that *People* magazine of hers to notice anybody walking by. We keep on east."

Tomzak grunted, but turned in the direction Macky wanted him to go. They were up to jogging speed in moments, moving past the mouth of Pierson Lane without a glance. Then a voice came out of the gloom and stopped them in mid-stride.

"Hey! You guys blind or what?"

It was Sister Matty coming out of the lane. Her hair was wind-blown, and she was breathing hard as if she'd just run a sprint. But she was all in one piece. The two men surrounded her, all smiles.

"Hey, Matty, you had us going for a few minutes there," Macky said. "Are you okay?"

She ignored him and, hands on hips, said to Tomzak, "Where the hell were you?"

CHAPTER 11

"Jesus—excuse me, Sister. But I mean, he grabbed you?"

"Pulled me into a doorway and tried to put the fear of the Lord into me. He pretty much succeeded too. I know we're all God's creatures, but what a disgusting creature this Carl person turned out to be."

"That son of a bitch—sorry, Matty. I get my hands on the dude he's gonna be even more disgusting. Did he hurt you?"

"He made things very uncomfortable for a couple of very long minutes. But no damage done, if we don't count nightmares."

"That dirty bastard—oops."

A lopsided grin appeared. "It's all right, gentlemen. I'm struggling with a few impure thoughts of my own just now."

They were seated in a booth at The Acropolis Diner: Sister Matty, Reuben Macky, and Chet Tomzak. Tomzak and

Macky had wanted to head back to the church right away, to let the others know Matty had been found. But the gritty little nun had wanted to talk first, just the three of them.

"First the facts." She knitted her fingers together. "We now know this man Carl has been blackmailing Father Joe. We also know he lives somewhere in the neighborhood, probably within two blocks of where we're sitting."

Macky took out a cigarette. "Makes sense. An alkie like that, he's not gonna be catching no cross-town buses. He'll be local."

"Correct. We don't know exactly where he's living, but with enough manpower we could probably find him soon enough. Either us or the police." She paused. "The question is, do we want to find him?"

"Yes," Tomzak said, surprised. "Of course we do. We have to find him."

"To prove your innocence," Matty said.

"Yeah, that. And because if we don't, he'll just keep on blackmailing Father Joe. Maybe attack him again if Joe doesn't come across."

Macky was nodding. "We need to confront this trash, let him know what'll happen to him if we see his ugly face around here again. We put a boot up his—backside, he'll most likely get out of town."

"And if he calls the police on you instead?" Matty asked. "You get caught assaulting him, and your parole would be automatically revoked, Reuben. The same goes for any of our men."

"So we hand what we have over to Hafner and Greene," Tomzak said. "Maybe they'll surprise us and do their jobs." But he had been watching her closely the whole time. He knew she had something else on her mind. "You asked if we really want to find Carl. What'd you mean, Matty?"

She played with her spoon, took a sip of her coffee, let out a sigh. It was all meant to give her a moment to think about her answer. "That's why I wanted to do this alone, just us three. It's not that I don't trust the other men, but—" Then she simply said it, straight out. "I think this Carl is blackmailing Father Joe over a killing that happened when he was a young man back in Chicago."

Tomzak groaned. Macky swore under his breath. When they quieted down again, she went on. "Carl gave me a message: 'Tell Joe he'd better be there tonight with my money. Everybody else paid for that killing and now it's his turn.'"

It was as if the air had been sucked from the booth. No one spoke, no one touched the coffee. Traffic rolled by out on Carson Avenue. From the kitchen came the sound of the fry cook arguing in Greek with the counterman.

Finally Sister Matty said, "Well, we can't sit here all day, gentlemen. Even if the coffee didn't taste like crankcase oil."

"Man," Macky said, exhaling a cloud of smoke.

"Yeah," Tomzak said. "Talk about a rock and a hard place."

"If we go to the cops, we could be signing a warrant on Father Joe," Macky said. "On the other side, if we let this Carl guy walk, chances are he'll come back at Joe for more money somewhere down the line."

"And if he doesn't pay," Tomzak added, "the guy calls the newspapers with whatever he's got on Father Joe. So it comes out anyway."

"So what do we do, gentlemen?"

Neither man wanted to answer until Macky said, "You know, I can't really believe Joe Costello went out and killed somebody. Not even when he was a kid. It's just not in him."

"I can't see it, either," Matty said. "But *something* bad happened, that's for certain. I think he's on a guilt trip, one that he's been living with for years. And I don't think he'll ever get past it until he faces up to whatever it was. The problem is, I also don't think he's yet willing to face up to it. Not unless he's given no choice."

Macky frowned. "You saying you think we should force the issue? Go to the cops?"

Matty smiled kindly. "I'm saying confession is good for the soul, Reuben, as any good Catholic knows."

*   *   *

They made a strange trio, sitting side by side at the interview table in I-Room 3. The nun, the tough black ex-con, and the nervous white ex-con. Sergeant Hafner figured they could have their own TV show, *The Mod Squad Gets Religion*.

He moved his styrofoam coffee cup two inches and rested his elbows on the table. "Is that it? All of it?"

"All of it?" Sister Matthew repeated innocently, then glanced at Tomzak.

He pretended not to notice. "That's the whole story," he said, saving Matty from having to lie.

It wasn't much of a lie. All they'd left out was Carl's comment about a killing. They had discussed it some more on the ride over to Metro Police Headquarters. They decided that it was best to hold back that one piece of information.

"I think we should keep any talk of murder to ourselves for as long as possible," Matty had said. "We want the police focused on Carl, not on Father Joe."

While Matty and Tomzak explained everything they'd learned about the man who had attacked Father Joe, Sergeant Hafner had listened closely. Sergeant Greene, in the meantime, had taken detailed notes on a white legal pad.

On the way down to police headquarters, they had all three agreed they were doing the right thing. Now as they sat there in silence waiting for Hafner to speak, they were each having second thoughts. Something to do with the way the sergeant studied their faces when they spoke.

Like he knew they were holding back on him.

Tomzak ended the silence. "So, uh, what happens now?"

Hafner shifted his eyes to him. "What happens?"

"How do you proceed? I guess you'll go out and find this Carl guy, right?"

"Oh, yeah." A sarcastic smile spread across Hafner's beefy face. "Me and Sergeant Greene here, we'll drive right over to the East End and canvas all the boardinghouses and flops and gin joints, see if we can't turn this guy up. There's only about a couple hundred places he could be living, so it'll take a week or two. But we got nothing better to do, right, Kel?"

"Nobody expects you to do it by yourselves," Sister Matty said. "You have a lot of uniformed officers who can—"

"Who are busy going out on their regular calls, ma'am," Greene said. "It's Saturday. In a few hours this place will be overflowing with wife beaters and drunken brawlers."

"And it ain't exactly open and shut, either," Hafner said. "Even if everything you've told us is true—" He held up his palm to ward off their protests. "—and I'm sure it is. But even so, what we've got is a priest who says he can't ID his attacker. Who doesn't even wanna press charges. And you don't even have a last name on this guy. A tall guy named Carl, that's it."

Tomzak shook his head in disbelief. "So you're not going to do anything?"

"C'mon, Sister," Macky said, starting to rise. "We can find this bum on our own."

"I wouldn't if I were you," Hafner said. "That would be interfering in a police investigation, which could put you right back in Arcadia."

"Hah. What police investigation would that be?"

"The one Sergeant Greene and I are handling."

"You just said—"

"I just said we wouldn't be out looking for Tall Carl this afternoon. That's because we don't have to." Hafner waited a beat, then smiled. "You know, for a bunch of budding Sherlock Holmeses, you people don't catch on too quick. You wanna clue them in, Kel?"

Greene tucked away his pen inside his suitcoat. "You said your man Carl is expecting another payment from Father Costello tonight. Which means they'll be meeting together somewhere, right?"

Tomzak nodded. He was beginning to see the light. "You can pick him up then. But we don't know where or exactly when they're planning to—"

"We don't have to," Greene said. "Father Costello knows the details of the meeting. All we have to do is tail him."

Now all three were nodding in approval—Macky, Tomzak, and Sister Matty.

"That's a very good plan, Sergeant," she said. "It never even occurred to me."

"Imagine that," Hafner said. "Well, I guess that's why they pay us professional detectives the big bucks."

CHAPTER
12

It was the stinking cold weather.
He couldn't take it anymore. God, he remembered as a kid,
climbing on the mounds of snow piled up in Lincoln Park.
Playing for hours in the stuff. Those giant chunks of ice that
washed up on the Lake Michigan shoreline, looking like
sculpture. Hot cocoa in the skating shack for a dime.

He never gave two seconds thought to the cold in those days.
But that was thirty years ago. He'd spent too long down in
Florida. Damn blood had gone thin on him.

"Brrrr," he said to the night. "I'll be right back down there
soon. Real soon, and that's where I'll stay."

He could picture himself sitting under a palmetto down in
St. Pete, over by the public pier. Hot day with a cool bay breeze.

Must've been a fool coming north this time of year. But he'd
seen that article in the St. Pete Times *about urban churches*
around the country. How they struggle to survive in the inner
cities. And there it was, a big picture of Joey Costello, all grown

up now. A priest, running his own church, ministering to the
down and out.

Oh, baby, he remembered thinking. The son of a bitch is doing
okay, inner city or no inner city, and he owes me. Owes me big.

"Ahh-choo." He found a tissue deep in the pockets of his
raincoat and swiped at his nose. Then he leaned out over the
railing and spit. He didn't bother to see if it hit the sidewalk or
the river, not that it mattered. Nobody crazy enough to be
hanging around down on that sidewalk in a cold drizzle.

He was playing it smart this time, being up on that bridge.
That little nun following him had got him thinking. If Joe had
her tailing him . . .

That's when he'd thought things through again and made his
decision. He'd make the score tonight, take the priest for as much
as he could get. Then he'd head back south for sure. There was
no point hanging around. He could blackmail Costello just as
good by phone.

He'd take what he could take tonight and head back to the
palm trees. Only he wasn't a fool. If the priest was trying to set
him up, he needed to be ready. So after he'd let the little nun go,
he called Joey again, changed the place for the meeting.

He didn't even know the name of the river that ran under
him, only that the bridge was called the 24th Street Bridge. And,
more important, that the public sidewalk ran underneath it,
along the riverbank. That's why he'd picked it for the meeting;
because up where he was, he could see anyone coming for two
blocks in either direction.

Yes, sir, Carl Moody was nobody's fool. He'd get his money
this time, that was for damn sure.

He pulled his collar tighter. Then he plunged his hands deep
into the pockets of the raincoat, where his right hand settled
around the cold comfort of the bone-handled jackknife.

*   *   *

Father Joe Costello hurried down Reliant Street, turning right at the corner. It was almost 9:15 and he was running late. The restaurant was as busy as he'd ever seen it on a Saturday night. That was good, of course. But on this particular Saturday night, every minute seemed to drag by.

"Am I wrong?" he asked God as he walked. "Tell me, please. Is there a greater good here, Father, or am I simply lying to myself?"

For that was the thing that cut him the deepest. The thought that none of this was really about his church, his ministry, carrying on for his people. He worried that it was all only to protect himself. To keep his secret hidden, so he wouldn't have to face up to the shame. Face up to losing the thing that meant everything to him: his parish.

He reached 24th Street. Even from two blocks away, he could hear the low rush of the river's high spring runoff. Other than a few far-off car horns, it was the only sound. Not much life in the East River district after dark.

It had been easier this time, getting the thousand. All he had to do was pocket it a bit at a time whenever he moved extra cash from the register to the lockbox in the storage room. No one would miss the money tonight.

Of course, there could be a question later on, when he and Macky and Tomzak went over the books for the restaurant. But he could handle that too. Extra funds were taken out of the restaurant's profits to help one of the other programs, he could say. They wouldn't argue; the budget was his responsibility, after all. It was a piece of cake.

Listen to him! Like some two-bit gangster congratulating himself for how cleverly he robbed the poor box.

He was almost there. Not fifty feet ahead, the bridge span soared like the arched back of a huge gray whale. He felt like Jonah about to enter its mouth. His pace slowed as he came closer. Indeed, the sidewalk disappeared under the bridge into a place every bit as dark as the whale's mouth.

He came to a stop twenty feet from the overhanging bridge and wiped the cold mist from his brow.

"God, give me the courage—"

"Hey, Joey. What're you doing, saying a prayer?"

He almost jumped out of his skin, hearing that whispered voice float down from above. For a split second, he almost thought—but no. The Lord may move in mysterious ways, but this was pushing things.

He looked up into the gloom but couldn't see beyond the halo cast by the street lamp. "Where are you, Carl?"

"Up here on the bridge, Joey. C'mon up. There's some stairs on the side there."

The concrete steps were steep and slick. Father Joe took his time in his hard-soled shoes. He found Carl on the bridge's sidewalk, sheltering from the wind behind one of the steel struts that formed the bridge's frame.

"You got my money?"

It was more a demand than a question. He already had his hand out, the fingers crabbed from the cold. Father Joe reached into his coat and came up with the roll of bills, held with a rubber band. Carl's watery eyes widened with glee when he saw the wad all those tens and twenties made.

He reached out. "Give it over."

"One last chance, Carl," Father Joe said, pulling back slightly. "It doesn't have to be like this. I can help you take hold of your life again. Give you a job, even. You could enroll in our alcohol dependency program—"

"Shove your programs, priest! I told you before I wasn't buying it."

"Think about it. You wouldn't have to live hand to mouth. We could—"

"Give me my goddamn money *now!*"

Father Joe didn't see the knife come out of Carl's coat. What he would remember was the sudden arc of Carl's arm and the slight tug of the blade as it cut through his wool sleeve. He didn't even realize he'd been cut at first.

"My money! I'll kill you, you bastard, if you don't give me my money!"

Suddenly the bridge was washed in light. Carl and Father Joe both jerked their heads from side to side, bewildered, even as a voice cut the air like a lightening bolt.

"THIS IS THE POLICE. STOP WHAT YOU'RE DOING AND DO NOT MOVE. THIS IS THE POLICE."

Father Joe heard a whimper escape from Carl. But when he turned back to face him, Carl was already running.

"STAY WHERE YOU ARE. I REPEAT, THIS IS THE POLICE."

Son of a bitch, son of a bitch, son of a bitch, son of a bitch.

Carl kept repeating it like a mantra as he ran across the 24th Street Bridge. There was no room in his addled brain for Father Joe or the money or anything else now. No. Only escape. Had to get away. Couldn't do time, not again. Not in some freezing goddamn Northern prison, make you go cold turkey in there, no booze, no palm trees, no, no, no—

He stopped short as car headlights raced toward him from the other side of the bridge. Cop lights, red and blue bar on top, a spot on the side, searching for him.

He was boxed. They had him trapped on the— no, no, no, no. Not if he could— could what?

He grabbed the cold iron railing and looked over the side. Thirty feet below, the river with no name raced and churned. But he was looking higher, at a narrow ledge of steel a few feet below the railing. If he could get down onto that ledge and work his way over toward the sidewalk at the far end of the bridge . . .

"YOU ON THE BRIDGE. DO NOT MOVE. KEEP YOUR HANDS IN SIGHT."

He got one leg over, lowered himself slowly to the ledge. There! He made it. Step by step, hand over hand. Careful, careful.

It wasn't so bad. He could make it, he could do this. Go as far as the bank on the other side and drop down, take off along the sidewalk. Run and keep running, out to the railyards and back down South. Down to warm sun and palm trees and all those fat guilty tourists.

Almost there. Another twenty feet. Ignore the sounds of the cops swarming the bridge. You're almost there, Carl boy, almost . . .

But then his cramped hand lost its grip and his knees began to quake. Suddenly he was leaning backward, windmilling his arms, trying to fly back to his ledge but falling. Falling like a stone, not even able to hear his own scream above the sirens. Falling against the rocks of the breakwater wall and bouncing like a rag doll into the freezing chop of the river.

*   *   *

Father Joe walked slowly out of the emergency surgery at St. Mary's and took a seat in the waiting area. With the bandage on his head and the new one on his upper arm, he looked worse than some of the patients.

"Is he—?" Sister Matty asked tenderly.

Father Joe shook his head. "He's on a respirator. They say he probably won't last the night, though. I administered the last rites, but I don't think he even knew I was there."

When the police fished Carl from the river, he was half frozen, he had a broken neck, and the back of his head was cracked like an egg. When they wheeled him into the emergency room, the attending doctor said he was still breathing, which was a miracle.

Sergeant Greene had notified Sister Matty of the situation. She and the others—Reuben Macky, Billboard, and Chet Tomzak—had arrived at the hospital only a few minutes behind the ambulance.

"It wasn't your fault, Joe," Macky said.

"Yeah," Billboard agreed. "Better him than you."

Father Joe leaned over and rested his face in his hands. He was too tired to raise his head and too ashamed to look at their faces anyway. "If I had been stronger at the start, this never would've gotten this far. If I'd faced the truth from the beginning—"

"Psst, cool it, Father," hissed Billboard as the two sergeants came down the hallway.

For once, Hafner seemed to have lost some of his swagger, Tomzak thought. Hafner and Greene both grabbed chairs, and the senior partner held up a sheet of computer paper.

"Carl Moody, age forty-eight—guy looked sixty, if you ask me. Did time in the late Sixties as a juvie in Chicago, a gang-related manslaughter rap. Graduated to the big time in the Seventies when he did a dime at Joliet for armed assault. There's half a dozen arrests since for minor stuff like DUI, shoplifting, mostly down in Florida."

He studied the priest for a moment. "Chicago is your hometown too, isn't it, Father?"

"Hey, why don't you leave him alone," Macky said. "The man's worn out."

"Yeah," Billboard said. "He don't have to talk if he don't want to."

"I guess that's true. Moody's not about to tell us anything, is he? So I guess your secret's safe, Father. If that's how you wanna leave it."

Father Joe looked up. His calm gaze rested on Sergeant Hafner before panning to Sister Matty and the others, lingering on Chet Tomzak. His soul brother in guilt, he thought, almost smiling.

Then he took a deep breath and let it all out.

We grew up off Belmont Avenue on the north side of Chicago, couple blocks from Lincoln. It was a good place really. You had Wrigley Field in one direction, the Lincoln Park Zoo in the other. The lakeshore was nearby. All in all, it was a good place to grow up.

But when you're a teenager, sometimes you can't see the good things, the simple pleasures. All you see is the broken glass and the broken homes, the broken dreams. My big brother Michael fell in with some of the neighborhood toughs. The truth is, he was one of the leaders. Carl Moody, he was just one of the gang, a hanger-on.

I loved my brother and admired him. Our father was a drunk who deserted us when I was nine. It was Michael who taught me how to play ball. And, I'm afraid, how to steal clothes from Marshall Fields and bust into parking meters.

When I was sixteen, we got called out by another gang. It was stupid stuff. I don't even remember what caused it. Anyway, we were to meet on neutral turf, this alley behind an empty warehouse. We heard this other gang had zip guns—turns out they didn't. But we didn't know that, so Michael made up some Molotov cocktails with ketchup bottles.

We got to the alley first and climbed up on one of the roofs. When the other gang showed up, Michael had us light up our Molotov cocktails and throw them down at their car, this old Buick. Nobody got hurt, none of the other boys anyway, but the warehouse started on fire. It burned to the ground. And a man who was sleeping in it, a derelict, burned to death.

The police eventually found out what happened from the other gang. Michael and Carl Moody were arrested and charged with arson and second degree manslaughter, along with two other guys from our gang. But Michael got everyone to leave my name out of it. I was never charged with anything.

Anyway, Michael went to prison for three years. After he got out, he got into more trouble and went back to prison again. He never came out. He was killed, knifed by another inmate, when he was twenty-seven years old.

I joined the seminary a year after the fire, but I never could forget what we'd done or that I'd never paid a price for it. Michael paid for me. And Moody and the others did too. Now, finally, I guess it's my turn.

When Father Joe finished, Sister Matty was quietly sobbing into a tissue. The others were dry-eyed but somber. All of them were looking at Sergeant Hafner, waiting for him to make the next move. Slowly he stood up.

"You get all that written down, Sergeant Greene?"

Greene shook his head ruefully. "I'm afraid my pen is out of ink, sergeant."

"Damn," Hafner said, shaking his head. "Then I guess we're just going to have to forget about the whole damn thing."

Father Joe's face went slack with disbelief. "That's it? You're not going to—?"

"Arrest you? Punish you? I think you've probably punished yourself better than any judge could." Hafner glanced at his partner, who was watching him with a small smile on his face. "The thing is, Father, we figure you spend your life giving mugs like these a second chance in life. Maybe it's time you practice what you preach, huh?"

"Oh, Sergeant!" Sister Matty jumped up and rushed over to him, wrapping her arms around his waist and hugging him. "Thank you, thank you."

"Jesus Christ," he muttered, staring down helplessly at the top of her head. "I was afraid this would happen."